Sow Death,
Reap Death

Also by Hugh Pentecost

Sow Death, Reap Death

HUGH PENTECOST
A Red Badge Novel of Suspense

DODD, MEAD & COMPANY, New York

1 2 3 4 5 6 7 8 9 10

Library of Congress Cataloging in Publication Data

Pentecost, Hugh, 1903–
    Sow death, reap death.

    (A Red badge novel of suspense)
    I. Title.
PS3531.H442S6   813'.52   81-9712
ISBN 0-396-08006-5   AACR2

Part One

1 "You have been fantasy seduced about eight dozen times since we walked in here," Quist said to his lady.

"Exclusive privileges for you only, my love," the lady said.

"Change that, even for a moment, and when I get back I will slit your lovely throat," Quist said.

They were a sensational-looking couple: Lydia Morton, dark, luscious, wearing an off-the-shoulder Givenchy black evening gown, and Julian Quist, tall, slender, golden-blond, looking like a Greek Apollo carved on a coin, elegant in a wine-red dinner jacket. Put them down in an extravagant restaurant like the Stirrup Cup, patronized only by the very rich and the very famous, and they attracted more attention than the most glamorous movie stars, or the princes and princesses of New York's social whirl. Quist was envied by other men, and Lydia by other women. There was something like regret in that envy because there was obviously no hope for anyone else with either of them. They were not married, but they lived together, quite openly, in a duplex apartment on Beekman Place. They were also partners in a business enterprise called Julian Quist Associates, perhaps the top public relations firm anywhere. They were in love, enduringly, permanently.

On this night, they had enjoyed a supper of lobster Newburg in a sauce seasoned with imported German beer, a dessert of brandied peaches, accented by a bottle of French champagne. When Quist rose, picked up Lydia's hand, and kissed the tips of her fingers, neither of them could have dreamed that they might be looking into each other's eyes for the last time ever.

"Beware of the wolves," Quist said.

He had no idea of the nature of the wolves that would threaten her.

For the last three years Julian Quist Associates had been heavily involved with a venture called the Island Complex. It was a sports center, twenty-five minutes from Penn Station on the Long Island Railroad. There was the main arena building, which housed fights, hockey games, basketball games, horse shows, dog shows, rodeos, circuses, and the business offices. Then there was the race track, competing with Aqueduct, Belmont, and Saratoga. That summer a stadium that would seat eighty thousand people was nearing completion; football, soccer, and track meets would be on view. "Olympics in 1984" was the slogan.

Julian Quist's closest friend and associate in their business was Dan Garvey, dark, volatile, a former All-American and professional football star until a knee injury ended his playing career. Sports were Garvey's primary interest in life, aside from women, and he was the ideal man to handle the promotion for the Complex. He maintained an office in the arena building, and on this night Quist and Lydia had come out to the Complex, supped at the fabulous Stirrup Cup, because Garvey had a promotion scheme to discuss with Quist and some members of the Complex's management committee.

"Sorry to drag you here at this time of night," Garvey said, when Quist arrived. "Only time we could get everyone together. You leave Lydia at the Cup?"

Quist nodded, looking past his friend at three well-dressed, expensive-looking gentlemen.

"It must be nice to have a girl you can leave alone," Garvey said.

"She won't be alone long," Quist said, smiling. "I heard a dozen chairs being pushed back from tables as I left the restaurant."

4

"Marvelous to have a girl you can trust," Garvey said.

"Quite marvelous," Quist said.

Quist knew the three other men in the office by sight and by name: banks, oil, steel. They controlled the Complex's multimillion-dollar budget. Quist knew why he was here. These men were going to need some selling to get them to approve Garvey's promotional plans.

Garvey had said it would take a half an hour. It took considerably more than that. Men with all the money in the world are hard to sell. That's why they have all the money in the world. Quist had been pressuring on Garvey's behalf for more than an hour when the door to Garvey's office burst open, without ceremony, and Vic Lorch, the big, dark-haired head of the Complex's security force, charged in.

"There's a big hell to pay," Lorch said. "Some guerrillas have taken over the Stirrup Cup. They're holding over two hundred guests and more than a hundred bartenders, waiters, and kitchen crew as hostages."

Quist started for the door. "Lydia's in there," he said.

Lorch blocked his way. "Hold it, Julian," he said. "They sent Mike Romano out." Romano was the manager of the Stirrup Cup. "There are thirty-five or forty of them, armed to the teeth. They've got the place mined with explosives. Any show of force from the outside and they'll blow the Stirrup Cup into the ocean! They showed Romano."

"What do they want?" The questioner's name was Broadhurst. He was steel.

"Money," the man named Coleman said. He was banks.

"What else?" the man named Fairchild said. He was oil.

"We don't know," Lorch said. "They told Romano they would call here to make their demands. I guess they knew the control of the money was meeting here."

"My wife is in there, too," Broadhurst said. That was his second thought.

"All we can do is sit tight," Lorch said. "We've notified the state police, the local cops. I've called Captain Haller of New York City Police's hostage negotiating team. He's an expert at this kind of squeeze. He's on his way."

"So what do we do?" Coleman asked.

"Wait," Lorch said, his mouth a grim slit. "That's all we can do."

Other people were crowding in the doorway, among them Mike Romano. Quist knew him well.

"How bad is it, Mike?" he asked.

"They've got everything," Romano said. "Machine pistols, hand grenades. There's a guy sitting in my office with a detonator. All he's got to do is get nervous and we've got more than three hundred dead people on our hands. They showed me. Explosives everywhere."

"Who are they?"

"Mixed bag," Romano said. "Men, women, kids, whites, blacks. I want to tell you, a teen-aged kid waving a machine pistol at our customers is a pretty scary sight."

"Lydia—Miss Morton?" Quist asked.

"I'm sorry, Mr. Quist. I was in my office when they burst in on me. I was taken, at gun point, on a tour of the kitchen and the basement areas where they've planted explosives. They hurried me upstairs and past the dining rooms after that. People were still at their tables, surrounded by a ring of goons with guns. I didn't happen to notice Miss Morton. But I don't think any of the guests were hurt. One of my chefs, who took a swing at one of these creeps with a meat cleaver, got shot in the shoulder." Romano shook his head. "Whole thing was well planned. The head man, the one in charge, actually had dinner at the Cup with a lady friend. Made a reservation days ago in the name of—for God's sake—John Smith. He was there, waiting for his army when they came—ready to take charge."

Garvey and the three Complex committeemen had gathered around to listen.

6

"You can describe this guy, Mike?" Garvey asked.

Romano shrugged. "Ordinary looking, black tie. Dark hair, dark glasses. I remember thinking that was odd at night—but a lot of people wear them these days, even after dark."

"Seen him before?" Garvey asked.

"Not that I remember. But hundreds of people come and go every night, Mr. Garvey."

Quist found himself remembering an old Groucho Marx insult.

"I never forget a face, but I'll try to make an exception in your case."

When there was crime in the air Quist thought of his good friend Lieutenant Mark Kreevich of Manhattan Homicide. Kreevich would know the best ways and the best people to handle this kind of situation. Quist headed for the telephone on Garvey's desk, but Vic Lorch blocked his way again.

"Don't use the phone, Julian. They may call any minute with whatever their demands are."

A cold anger was clutching at Quist. Lydia! She must be frightened out of her wits. He couldn't just wait here and do nothing. He glanced at his watch.

"The last race will be over at the track in about twenty minutes. What happens then, Vic?" he asked the security man. "Normally a crowd of people head for the Stirrup Cup and drink for the road."

"We've got the area roped off," Lorch said. "My twenty men and a dozen state troopers will keep people out."

"Then the news will spread like a forest fire and there'll be hundreds of curiosity hounds and rubberneckers," Quist said.

"More like a few thousand," Lorch said. "Some crazy bastards try to break in and we've had it. I've got a loudspeaker system set up and more troopers are on the way."

The phone on Garvey's desk rang. Garvey moved quickly. On his desk was a squawk box, attached to the phone, so that everyone in the office could be in on a conversation. Garvey gestured for silence, switched on the box, and picked up the phone.

"Dan Garvey here."

"Good evening, Mr. Garvey." It was a smooth, cultivated voice. "I trust you have your conference-call box connected, because I am only going to tell you what I want once."

"Who are you?"

"You can call me the Voice," the man said. He sounded amused.

"Or John Smith?"

"You pays your money and you takes your choice, Mr. Garvey. Just know that I'm in command of what's going on here at the Stirrup Cup."

"What are your terms? How much?" Garvey asked.

"I know it will surprise the people with you, particularly Messrs. Broadhurst, Coleman, and Fairchild. I don't want money. I want two people delivered to me here, alive and well."

"What two people?"

"Number one," the Voice said, "is Judge Stephen Padgett of the criminal court system in Manhattan. Number two is Carl Zorn, who prosecuted Paul Kramer a few months back in Judge Padgett's court."

The names seemed to mean nothing to anyone in the room except Vic Lorch.

"This is Vic Lorch, security," Vic said.

"I congratulate you on using your head so far, Mr. Lorch," the Voice said.

"Paul Kramer was involved in some kind of cult violence in the city, right?"

"And hanged himself in his jail cell about three weeks

8

ago," the Voice said, "having been sentenced to life imprisonment by Judge Padgett, after being convicted on false evidence presented by Carl Zorn. We are Paul Kramer's friends. Have you ever heard of the Reapers, Mr. Lorch?"

"That was what Kramer's cult friends called themselves."

"Right." The Voice had turned cold. "Sow death, reap death. The judge and Carl Zorn sent a good man to his death. We will try them, find them guilty, and execute them. You will deliver them to us, gentlemen, within a reasonable time, or we will begin to send out dead hostages in the trash."

"Do you expect the judge and the prosecutor to turn themselves over to you voluntarily in order to save the people you're holding prisoner?" Quist heard himself ask in a flat voice.

"That's Julian Quist, isn't it?" the Voice asked. "I was sitting at the next table to you in the Cup a little while ago. I recognize your voice. You're worried about your lovely lady, aren't you?"

"You sonofabitch," Quist said, quite quietly.

"To answer your question, Mr. Quist, it's up to you people to persuade Judge Padgett and Mr. Zorn that they hold the lives of three hundred and twenty-seven people in their hands."

"My wife is in there," Broadhurst called out. "Surely you could use some money. One person can't make so much difference."

"There's only one price for the freedom of anyone," the Voice said. "Bring us the judge and Carl Zorn. That's it, without argument. I know it can't be managed in an instant. There is food enough in the freezers, and lockers, and pantries here to keep us going for quite a spell. Call me on Mr. Romano's private phone tomorrow morning at ten. Not before that, because there is no point in trying to make

9

any other deal. Let me know then how you are progressing. Good evening, gentlemen."

"Smith!" Garvey shouted.

The dial tone sounded through the squawk box.

"The man is preposterous!" Joel Broadhurst said. "Does he really think we can deliver people to him to be killed?"

Everyone began to talk at once.

"Your private phone number," Vic Lorch asked Romano.

Romano bent over the desk and scribbled the number on a message pad. "It's not unlisted," he said. "It's just a line I keep for personal calls, so that I don't get cluttered up with reservations and other restaurant business."

Lorch dialed the number and waited. Busy.

"He meant what he told us," Garvey said. "Ten o'clock in the morning."

"We're going to be swarmed over by people from the media—press, radio, TV," Lorch said. "Can you handle them, Dan?"

Garvey nodded. "Do we tell them what this crazy wants?"

"I imagine the Voice will handle his own publicity," Quist said. "There's going to be pressure from hundreds of relatives and friends for us to do something. That's the way he'll want it."

"Judge Padgett and Carl Zorn hear the news and they'll be off for the North Pole," Garvey said.

"They can't do that!" Broadhurst said.

"What would you do, Mr. Broadhurst, if they asked for your neck on the block?" Garvey asked.

"I'd tell them to —" Broadhurst didn't go on.

"And to hell with three hundred and twenty-seven people," Garvey said. "They can send us out a body an hour for the next two weeks!"

"They wouldn't dare!" Broadhurst said.

10

"Try praying," Garvey said.

Quist couldn't listen to any more of that. He turned and walked out of the office, out into a moonlit summer night. Across the massive, paved parking lot the racetrack was lighted, bright as day, the track announcer's voice droning out the call of a race over the public loudspeaker, the crowd cheering excitedly as the horses turned into the stretch. Thousands of people there were totally unaware that a bizarre violence was taking place only a few hundred yards away. After the last race most of them would just go to their cars or to the special trains and buses and head for home without having any notion of it. How long before the Voice got his message to the media and the attention of the entire country would be focused on the Stirrup Cup and the Island Complex? When that happened, Quist thought, they'd need more than a couple of dozen of Lorch's security men and a handful of cops to keep order. They'd need an army!

Through the vents in venetian blinds it was apparent that the main floor interior of the Stirrup Cup was still brightly lit, but the outside lights, normally focused on the sprawling building, had been extinguished. The paths leading from the parking lot and the arena building had been locked off and were guarded by state troopers. In a few minutes the last race would have been run at the track and scores of customers, prepared to buy a nightcap at the Stirrup Cup's bar, would be asking why the place had been closed so early.

Quist spotted a glassed-in public phone located on the rim of the parking lot and headed for it. His friend, Lieutenant Kreevich, was still on his mind. Kreevich was a new breed of cop, law degree, efficient in all the new and sophisticated techniques of crime fighting. He was a dark, wiry, energetic man whom Quist had encountered some years ago on a murder case with which they were both

11

concerned. The two men found they had mutual interests in the theater, the arts, sports. They liked each other on sight and became warm friends. Kreevich's jurisdiction was Manhattan. He thought of the city as the capital of the world, with the United Nations there, the center for world tourism, as a place where the top criminals from everywhere would eventually circulate. He complained that the police, by and large, only became involved with crime after it was committed. His personal aim was to prevent, not to solve. He was in constant touch with the police forces in all the metropolitan centers in this country and Europe. In an age when terrorism was becoming a daily commonplace, Mark Kreevich was committed to preventing it in his back yard. Technically, he was a Homicide man, but all terrorism involves murder. Kreevich was, Quist thought, perhaps already too late for this one, but he would have the best advice on what could be done.

There had to be some kind of luck on his side, Quist thought, as he dialed Kreevich's home phone in the city and waited.

Kreevich sounded sleepy. "Friend or foe?" he asked.

"It's Julian, Mark. Have you heard any startling news on your television set?"

"You know I don't watch television, chum, unless I have to."

"I'm out at the Complex, Mark. About an hour ago an army of people who call themselves the Reapers took over the Stirrup Cup and are holding over three hundred people hostage."

"You're kidding!" Kreevich was suddenly wide awake.

"I wish I was. Lydia is one of the hostages. According to Romano, the manager who was let out, they're armed with automatic weapons, grenades, and they've planted explosives all over the place."

"Do you know what they're asking for?"

"They've been in touch about fifteen minutes ago," Quist said. "It's not money. They want two people delivered to them—Judge Stephen Padgett of the criminal court and Carl Zorn, a federal prosecutor."

"Oh, brother!" Kreevich said. "Is Lydia okay?"

"Who knows? Romano thinks no one has been hurt—yet."

"Who's in charge?"

"State police, local cops, and Vic Lorch. You know him."

Kreevich had recommended Lorch when the Complex was looking for a security man.

"What are they doing?"

"Got the Cup blocked off. God knows what will happen when the crowd comes out of the racetrack. Lorch has been in touch with a Captain Haller who's supposed to know something about hostage negotiations."

"A first-rate man. You couldn't have better. But will they negotiate?"

"They say not. No money, no deals. According to the head man, they propose to try Padgett and Zorn, find them guilty, and execute them."

"You know anything about the Reapers?" Kreevich asked, his voice gone cold and hard.

"Lorch says they're some kind of cult."

"I know about them," Kreevich said. "They're high on my list, Julian. Fight terror with terror under the guise of religious justice. 'An eye for an eye.'"

"'Sow death, reap death,' the man said on the phone."

"That's the Reapers," Kreevich said. "Doing God's work with a machine gun! Ever hear of a man named Paul Kramer?"

"He was mentioned tonight."

"One of the top guys in the Reapers. He was charged with murdering a Justice Department lawyer. Zorn prosecuted. Padgett sentenced him to a life term. He hanged

13

himself in his cell at Attica about three weeks ago. Both Padgett and Zorn have been guarded ever since the trial. Authorities thought the Reapers might be out to get them. So they chose this way!"

"We deliver the judge and Zorn or they will start sending out bodies in the trash," Quist said. "We're to call them at ten o'clock in the morning and tell them how we're progressing. If we storm the joint, they'll blow it up with everybody in it."

"And they just might," Kreevich said. "They're fanatics, Julian. They are not afraid of death themselves. Look, chum. Sit tight. Do what Fred Haller advises. I'll be out there within the hour. And, Julian?"

"Yes?"

"Lydia is some kind of gutsy girl. She'll make it."

"Will any of them make it?" Quist said. For one of the few times in his life he knew fear—for Lydia.

Quist had been right about one thing. The man who called himself the Voice had not waited for anyone else to let the world know what the situation was at the Stirrup Cup. While Quist had been talking to Kreevich, the Voice had been in touch with the television networks, the radio stations, and the press. The Stirrup Cup was in the hands of the Reapers. Unless Judge Padgett and Carl Zorn were delivered to them within a reasonable time the hostages would be eliminated one by one. If any attempt was made to storm the Stirrup Cup, it would be blown to pieces with everyone in it.

While Quist stood outside the Stirrup Cup trying to make sense about what to do, phones in the complex were ringing everywhere. The networks, the newspapers, were greedy for information. Special bulletins were appearing on TV screens in a million homes and apartments; radios blared the news in city bars, in taxicabs and private cars. You would have to be asleep and out of touch with the world to miss knowing what had happened at the Complex.

Someone in authority had decided on a course of action. Quist could hear the loudspeaker at the track, calling for attention.

"Ladies and gentlemen, I have an emergency announcement to make. Terrorists have taken over the Stirrup Cup adjacent to the track here. They are holding over three hundred hostages and threaten to kill them if any move is made to enter the restaurant and bar. The management has decided to cancel the final race here." Quist could hear the thunder of thousands of voices. "Please! Please listen!" The voices faded. "State police and security forces have the Stirrup Cup surrounded. You are asked to leave in an orderly fashion and go to your cars, your buses, or trains and leave the situation in their hands. Any kind of individual attempt to do something can only cost lives. Your televisions and radios will keep you posted on what is happening. You are urged to leave quietly and quickly. Any kind of mob reaction can only lead to disaster. Thank you!"

Thousands of people began to pour out of the track grandstand, shouting questions, calling to friends. Whoever had given the order had guessed right. All but a few score of people headed for their transportation, moving slowly past the grim-faced cops and security guards who were blocking direct access to the Cup. People shouted questions at them, but if the cops replied their answers were lost in a babel of voices. People walked slowly, gawking at the darkened restaurant, but most of them kept moving. There are always people who refuse, on principle, to obey the rules; "Don't spit on the sidewalk" and they spit. There were others who had some connection with the Complex, employees at the track, maintenance people, a small army of clean-up people ready to go to work the minute the last crowd left, curious grooms, guards, stablehands from the Shed Row area beyond the track. To these

15

people their own property, the place where they worked and in which they had a stake, was being violated.

Quist felt a hand on his arm and turned. He found himself looking down at an attractive girl with dark red hair. She was wearing an evening dress, a light summer scarf drawn over bare shoulders. Dark eyes, wide with shock, questioned him. She was familiar, but for an instant he didn't place her.

"Sally Craven," she said.

"Of course," Quist said. "I'm sorry, Sally, I'm just not quite all together at the moment. My lady is inside that place."

"Miss Morton? Oh, I'm so sorry."

In his time hundreds of promising young entertainers had crossed Quist's path. They tried all kinds of ways to attract his attention, because if Julian Quist Associates could be persuaded to promote them they had it made. For the last couple of months Sally Craven had been in Quist's sights. She was singing in the Stirrup Cup, three shows a night—eight, eleven, and two A.M. Old show tunes, old standards, were her thing. With a very good man accompanying her, she just stood by the piano and in a low, throaty voice recalled for you all the tunes you had once loved. She was what Quist called a "parlor entertainer." She was at her best in a smallish room, casual, almost informal. Quist remembered as a small boy evenings in his parents' home when his father, on a party night, would say, "Maybe Miss So-and-so would sing something for us." And Miss So-and-so would sing, without any fanfare, without any show-business pizzazz. It was charming, but probably not big time; not a great voice, not a dazzling presence, just a simple charm. The core of Sally's act was in a little theme song she began her turn with: "I'm Just a Girl Who Can't Say No." And then she would ask, "What would you like to hear?" and the customers would call out song titles and she was underway. Pete Damon, who played the piano, knew everything, and Sally knew the lyrics to what must have been hundreds of songs. In its small, intimate way, it was first class.

"Pete's in there, too," Sally said.

"Your pianist?"

"Yes. I'd just finished my first turn—about nine-thirty, I guess. The room was terribly smoky and I walked out into the yard to get a little fresh air. Pete likes smoke and crowds. He went to the bar. Suddenly I saw—like an army—these men in ski masks rushing into the Cup with guns. I ran to find Vic Lorch—or someone—for help. I just heard what they said on the loudspeaker at the track. Do you think—my God, Mr. Quist, the people in there with those killers!"

"You were lucky you needed air," Quist said. "I suppose I was lucky, too. I had a business appointment in Dan Garvey's office and left Lydia behind."

Sally's fingers tightened on Quist's arm. "You'd rather be in there with her, wouldn't you?"

"I'm not certain I know where I could be the most use to her, inside or out," Quist said. "But I don't have a choice, do I?"

The girl looked confused. "My bag is in there in my dressing room," she said. "Money, credit cards, believe it or not, my lipstick!"

"You look fine," Quist said. "If you need taxi money—?"

"I can't just go off and leave Peter in there!" she said. "Can you, Mr. Quist? Just take a taxi and leave Miss Morton in there?"

"No."

"Then what *do* we do?"

"We wait for experts to tell us," Quist said. Waiting, he thought, was going to be the name of the game. For how long?

17

2   In the space of a short time the world was changed for thousands of people, not just the three hundred plus hostages surrounded by gun-waving, fanatical terrorists in the Stirrup Cup, but also for their families, friends, lovers, business associates. It was changed for policemen and security guards at the Complex. It was changed for people in authority. The FBI had been alerted, the National Guard. The mayor of New York, from where most of these people came, was trying to deal with a flood of appeals for action of some kind. The president in the White House had been informed of the situation. Of course the key figures in the deal demanded by the terrorists, Judge Stephen Padgett and Carl Zorn, the prosecutor, knew within minutes that their lives were on the line.

You couldn't make a phone call to or from the Island. The lines were overloaded, hopelessly backed up for no one could guess how long. The governor, the state's two senators, all kinds of state officials, were being bombarded with demands that they "do something." But what do you do? You wait for the experts to suggest, to assess the odds, to come up with psychological profiles of the terrorists so you'll have a notion of how to talk to them.

Captain Fred Haller, of the Manhattan Police, knew that it was guesswork, and gamble, and arriving at just the right time to do just the right thing—whatever that might be. And luck, he would tell anyone who asked him. He had spent most of his career as a police officer, talking would-be suicides off ledges on high buildings or bridges, dealing with robberies where hostages were taken to hold off police, talking reason to psychotics who were threatening the lives of wives and children, hijackers at airports holding whole planeloads of people and threatening their survival unless they were flown to Cuba or Iran or any other place where they would be safe from extradition. Haller's success in these situations had been consistent enough to keep luck from seeming to be a major factor.

"There has to be luck," he would insist. "There is just one note that will shatter the glass, and if you don't hit it–!"

Haller was young-looking, almost boyish, for a man forty-eight years old. He had sandy brown hair, compassionate gray eyes, and a pleasant smile that could freeze into a hard, straight line when things reached the touch-and-go stage. He was tall, slim, lanky, looking more like an amiable schoolteacher than a man who constantly bargained with killers and crazies for human survival.

The almost hysterical bedlam in Dan Garvey's office in the arena building was turned to silence when Captain Haller and three of his personal aides arrived.

"Someone take it from the top, please," Haller said.

Vic Lorch, the giant security chief, told of being alerted by Sally Craven, who was standing in the doorway with Julian Quist.

"Almost before I could organize anything they turned Mike Romano loose," Lorch said. "He's the manager of the Stirrup Cup. He'd seen their weapons, the explosives they've planted."

Haller turned to Romano. "You saw explosives?"

"Basement, kitchens, around the foundations," Romano said. "It must have been done well in advance—before they raided the place. There's a guy sitting in my office with a detonator, ready to blow everything sky high."

"They communicated with us here," Lorch said. "Told Romano they would. The one in charge told Romano his name was John Smith, but he calls himself the Voice. He told us on the phone what they wanted—Judge Padgett and Carl Zorn. He identified his people as the Reapers. I know they're some kind of cockeyed cult."

"I know about them," Haller said.

"I tried to get back to this Voice, but the phone is off the hook there. He'll talk to us at ten in the morning, not before."

Haller glanced at his watch. "A little less than nine hours," he said. "You did a good job clearing customers out, Mr. Lorch, but the media people are crowding in like swarming bees."

"The Reapers spread the word, not us," Lorch said. "I couldn't block the entrances to the grounds till we got people out. We've got experts here to handle the media people, though. Mr. Quist and Dan Garvey handle the promotion for the Complex. Dealing with news people is their business."

"I'm not going to be much good," Quist said from the doorway, a statue in a red dinner jacket. "My lady is in that hellhole out there. The only thing on my mind is murder!"

"A certain way to make sure you never see her again," Haller said. "There must be architect's plans for that building. It's only a few years old, isn't it?"

Romano's laugh was bitter. "There are plans, Captain— in my safe, in my office, in the building."

"You could sketch out a rough plan for me, couldn't you, Mr. Romano? Doors, windows, ventilators big enough for a man to crawl through, any kind of way in or out? We'll get formal plans from the architects when we can reach them."

"You thinking of trying to go in, Captain?" Vic Lorch asked.

Haller grinned at him. "In my business you make plans for anything that might happen at some time in the future. More important right now is to make certain none of them leave the building without our knowing. They've got the hostages, but we've got them. Containment, Mr. Lorch.

That's the first rule of the game. No coming and going—unless we choose to let someone go so we can follow him."

"This Voice, this John Smith, actually had dinner in the Cup," Lorch said. "Made his reservation several days ago, according to Romano. The whole thing is well planned, Captain."

"Of course it's well planned," Haller said. "The Reapers are professionals—at terror."

"Let me see if I understand the situation, Captain," Quist said from where he stood at the doorway with Sally Craven. His face looked carved out of rock. "No one in authority, on the outside, is going to consider for a minute turning over Padgett and Zorn to these creeps."

"No one," Haller said quietly.

"What happens when they start sending out dead hostages to us?"

"I like to think that's a long distance away," Haller said. "They want Padgett and Zorn badly. They have to know that once they start killing hostages the ball game is over. They've given us time, until ten in the morning. When we talk to their man, then we ask for more time. We'll get it. How much, who can say? How long can they keep eating and drinking in there, Mr. Romano?"

"Quite a while," Romano said. "Couple of weeks, maybe, if they handle it. They'll run out of fresh food in a few days, but there are quantities of canned and frozen stuff."

"So we have time to make them think we're trying to meet their demands," Haller said. "During that time we make our own plans."

"Such as?"

Haller shrugged. "First, we try to talk them out of it, try to make them see how impossible it is to do what they ask. That won't work, but it will give us time. Then we offer them some other kind of deal. Money. We could raise a small fortune for the hostages in that building. If they show any interest in that, which I doubt, we can offer them freedom—the chance to walk away with no hostages hurt, no terrorists hurt."

"But you don't think they'll buy that?" Quist asked.

"Not tomorrow morning at ten o'clock," Haller said. "Time and public responses of people in high places may work for us."

"But you don't believe that?"

"Look, Mr. Quist, you're not a reporter asking me questions," Haller said. "You're one of hundreds of people who have an enormous stake in this thing. Someone who matters to you is a hostage. I don't know any way to make that easy for you except to lie to you."

"So try the truth!"

"The truth isn't going to be easy to take, Mr. Quist," Haller said. "The Reapers are not gangsters looking for a way to get rich. They're not revolutionaries with political motives. They are a kind of religious fanatics. Mr. Romano has told you that in that building are whites, blacks, older people, teen-agers. One of their 'saints,' a man named Kramer, went to his death because of Padgett and Zorn. They're not looking for money, they're not looking for freedom, they're looking for their particular kind of justice. 'Sow death, reap death.' If they fail in that aim, the execution of two men we can't give them, they may choose to die themselves. The man in Romano's office will push down the plunger on his detonator and blow them all into eternity—hostages, terrorists, all of them."

"You're telling me there's no way we can win," Quist said.

"Not quite," Haller said. "In any religious or fraternal group there is always a Judas, or at least a Doubting Thomas. In other words, there is a weak spot. If we can find it, we have a chance. Not all the Reapers in existence are in that building. There are several thousand of them across the country, many of them in New York. Our chance, Mr. Quist, is finding someone on the outside who will sell out those people on the inside. My job is to gain all the time I can in negotiations with the Voice. The rest of you, the police, the FBI, everyone concerned, will use that time to try to find us a Judas."

"What can such a Judas do for us?" Quist asked.

"There is only one thing I can see," Haller said. "The people who are waving guns around in that building have got to lose faith in their leaders, the men who are giving the orders, the men who will ask them to die for their beliefs if necessary. Divide and conquer."

"So you find a Judas and there is something phony about the Voice or John Smith or whatever his name is. How do you persuade the others they're being misled?"

"My dear Mr. Quist," Haller said, "do you imagine those characters are not listening to every radio bulletin, every news show on television?"

"And if the Voice, John Smith, turns out to be as pure as the driven snow?"

"Why, that's where you come in Mr. Quist," Haller said, smiling. "Selling a bill of goods to the public, true or false, is your business, isn't it? Surely you can get cooperation from the networks to sell a lie, if that's what's needed to save three hundred or more lives."

"You believe that's the way to do it?"

"It may be a way," Haller said. "We have to be prepared for it if it comes to that. My men here, Sergeant Akleman and Officers Barton and O'Neil, will go back in the city looking for Reapers. They're probably all hidden away, now that this story has broken. But there is one man, Mr. Quist, who may know more about the Reapers than the members themselves. That man is Carl Zorn, who researched and built a winning case against Paul Kramer, the man this is all about."

"So why aren't we talking to him?" Quist asked.

"Because just at this moment we don't know where he is," Haller said.

Much later, when Quist tried to put down on paper the sequence of events at the beginning of the worst stretch of time in his life, he couldn't recall the exact order of things. Did Mark Kreevich arrive while Captain Haller was still spelling it out for them? He was certainly there when Rusty Grimes, top reporter for *Newsview* magazine, heading a delegation from the army of news people waiting outside, demanded facts, routines they were expected to follow. Was it while Grimes was there that the "sick man" was sent out of the Cup by the Reapers to deepen their anxiety with an account of what was going on inside the captured restaurant?

You aren't rational, Quist told himself, when you are personally involved in a crisis. Round and round, in the back of his head, revolved schemes for breaking into the Cup, through some back entrance, down some air vent, or through some crawl space below the roof. He would get to Lydia and snatch her out of there. He might even get to the detonator in Romano's office and deal with the creep who was there, prepared to blow the place up. He might even get to the Voice and silence that smooth-talking bastard.

"I haven't dreamed of being such a hero since I was eight years old and somebody broke into our house and stole my mother's jewel case," he said to Kreevich. "I was going to fight the whole world to get it back for her."

Kreevich was the rock of reason that he needed.

"Haller's right, Julian," the Homicide man said. "Time works for us for a while. Right now we have no way to bargain. Hours from now we may have found something."

"A Judas?"

24

"Who knows? Haller's men, Akleman and the others, are pretty shrewd operators. My money is on Carl Zorn, when we find him. He worked on the Reapers for months when he was building his case against Kramer."

"Why can't we find him? I thought someone said he was being guarded."

"Guarded, but not locked away. Wherever he is, when he hears the news he'll be in touch." Kreevich's pale blue eyes were touched with sympathy. "Like I said to you on the phone, Julian, Lydia is a gutsy girl. She'll see it through."

It was then that Rusty Grimes made his appearance on the scene, accompanied by two other reporters, Hal Linder from *International* and Helen Bates from the *Journal*. Quist knew all three of them quite well, top people at their trade. They'd been appointed a committee by the army of news people who were crowded around outside.

Rusty Grimes was a big bear of a man with brick-red hair, which accounted for his nickname. His peers thought of him as the best police reporter in the business. He nodded to Quist and Kreevich and waited for Captain Haller to turn away from his three assistants to whom he was giving instructions before they took off.

"Is it true your gal is in there, Julian?" Helen Bates asked. She was a brisk, very businesslike young woman who had made a reputation for herself covering the Holcomb kidnapping case a year or so ago.

"I don't think Captain Haller wants to release names yet, Helen," Kreevich said. "The list is still too incomplete. But, off the record, Lydia Morton is one of the hostages."

"They're crazy people!" Helen said.

"Amen," Quist muttered.

"The word we got from the character in charge is that there are over three hundred hostages," Helen said.

25

"Three hundred and twenty-seven is their figure," Kreevich said. "We don't have a head count of our own, but that's not far off."

Captain Haller's three men made a quick exit from the crowded office and Haller turned to give Rusty Grimes his easy smile. "So, what can I do for you, Rusty?"

"Would you believe there are a couple of hundred reporters, cameramen, and commentators waiting outside to know where the hell we're at?" Rusty Grimes said.

"Looks like we've made the big time," Haller said. "I appreciate they're not all breaking in here. I can't tell them any more than they already know from the man inside who gave you the word. What he told you, he told us. You can talk to Mike Romano, the manager of the Cup, who was inside when they took over—after you've done with me. They turned Romano loose after they'd shown him where explosives were set so we'd know they weren't giving us a fairy story."

"How do we handle it without getting in your way?" Grimes asked.

"Number one, see to it that some enterprising jerk doesn't try to get in there," Haller said. "You can set up your cameras outside the ropes. You can talk to anyone who's on the outside. Romano will give your whole army a press conference. I guess what he has is what you call 'color,' right? But let me get something quite straight with you, Rusty. There are three hundred and twenty-seven hostages in that building, along with forty or fifty terrorists. We have no count on them, only Romano's guesstimate. If anybody tries anything that sets off anyone with a nervous trigger finger, it could blow the whole situation out of control."

"Are you in touch with them?" Grimes asked.

"Not really," Haller said. "We are to call them at ten in

26

the morning. We've had no luck trying to reach them since I got here. The phone is off the hook, or busy."

"What phone?"

"That's a line we have to keep clear, Rusty. We can't have you people clogging it up."

"So let's get down to the payoff, Captain," Grimes said. "You're obviously not going to turn Judge Padgett and Carl Zorn over to them"

"Obviously," Haller said.

"So what then?"

"Some other kind of deal," Haller said.

"What kind of deal?"

"I won't have any idea till I talk to them myself."

"They must know you can't come through for them."

"The stakes are high," Haller said. "Two for three hundred twenty-seven. They may be crazy enough to think we'll buy it."

"And we may have to!" Joel Broadhurst, the steel man, broke in. "My wife is in there."

"A lot of people's women are in there, Mr. Broadhurst," Haller said. "We can't buy them out with lives." He turned to Vic Lorch. "Is there someplace in this building where the reporters can meet with Mike Romano?"

"I'll set it up," Lorch said. He started to leave when the telephone on Garvey's desk rang.

Garvey switched on the squawk box and answered.

"I'd like to speak to Captain Haller," the smooth voice of the Voice came over the line.

The room was suddenly deathly silent as Haller took the phone from Garvey.

"Hello, Mr. Smith," he said.

"Glad to know you're on the job, Captain," the Voice said. "We only like to deal with the best."

"Should I feel flattered, Mr. Smith?"

"They know everything that's going on," Quist whispered to Kreevich. "They know who was in this office when they first called. They know Haller is here now. They must have someone on the outside."

"We have a problem in here, Captain," the Voice said. "A sick man. Heart condition, I think. He can't get his breath. I'm going to send him out the kitchen exit at the rear. Lorch can show you where it is. I don't want anyone in here dying of natural causes."

"Conditions?" Haller asked.

"No conditions, Captain, except—someone's going to have to help this man out and turn him over to you. That someone is going to have to come back in, untouched. You try to hold him, question him, and we'll deliver enough dead ones to you to keep you entertained for quite a while. Is that quite clear?"

"Quite," Haller said.

"I suggest you advise Mr. Grimes not to alert his eager friends out front. Surround this man we're sending out with an army of hysterical reporters and he may just pass out on you. In exactly ten minutes, Captain. Have someone at the kitchen exit."

The dial tone sounded.

Vic Lorch, followed by Quist, Kreevich, and Garvey, were on their way almost before Haller had put down the phone. Haller seemed satisfied to let them be the ones.

Lorch, running, led the way across an open area and around to the rear of the darkened restaurant. The four men stood there in the unlit area, waiting.

"There's a loading platform for trucks," Lorch told them. "They'll bring him out above ground level. A couple of us should go up there. You with me, Lieutenant?"

"Go," Kreevich said.

Quist, standing there with Garvey, watched the two

28

others disappear into the gloom. Then, a door opened onto the platform, which was suddenly visible because of brilliant lights behind it. Two men came slowly out from the inside, one of them with his arm draped around the shoulders of the other. This man's legs were rubbery under him. Across his eyes was some kind of blindfold. The man who supported him was wearing a dark suit and he had a black ski mask over his face.

"He's all yours, pals," the one in the ski mask said.

Lorch and Kreevich appeared in the light. Quist knew it was a good thing he hadn't gone up on the platform with Lorch. He wouldn't have been able to restrain himself. The temptation to clobber the man with the ski mask and charge on into the restaurant would have been too much.

Kreevich and Lorch supported the blindfolded man on each side and Ski Mask went back into the building. The door was closed and they were in pitch darkness again.

The man with the blindfold was gasping for breath.

"Oh my God, oh my God, oh my God!" he kept saying, strangling over the words.

Lorch had a flashlight. He turned it on the man's face.

"Easy, friend," he said. Then: "It's some kind of adhesive tape! It's going to hurt a little, mister, but—here goes!"

There was a little sob of pain from the man as the blindfold was ripped off his eyes.

"I'm going to hand down my torch, Dan," Lorch said. "Light the steps."

Garvey moved forward and the steps were lighted. Kreevich and Lorch crossed hands and made a kind of seat, lifting the man who draped an arm around each of them. He seemed able to cooperate. But he kept saying "Oh my God" over and over. They literally ran with him around the corner of the building and into a side entrance to Garvey's office, avoiding the army of reporters.

The light hurt the man's eyes as they put him down in a green leather chair. He bent forward, his head almost down to his knees, trying to suck in air.

"It's Mr. Fahnestock," Romano said. "David Fahnestock. He's a lawyer, I think. One of our regulars. Mr. Fahnestock! It's Mike Romano."

Fahnestock shook his head from side to side, still fighting for breath. After a moment or two he straightened up and looked around at the circle of faces.

"Thanks," he said, to whoever. "It—it's emphysema, not heart. But when I can't get my breath my heart beats so fast they thought—" He took a deep breath, exhaling through pursed lips.

"Take your time, Mr. Fahnestock," Haller said. "I'm Captain Haller, in charge here."

"Christ Almighty, what can you do?" Fahnestock said.

"Maybe you can help us when you've got your breath," Haller said.

"It doesn't get much better than this," Fahnestock said. "I keep oxygen at home, but—"

"There's oxygen in my office—for emergencies," Lorch said, and went out again.

"Can you tell us, Mr. Fahnestock," Haller asked, "if you were blindfolded to bring you out, or before that?"

Fahnestock shook his head from side to side. Speaking a sentence seemed to exhaust him.

"Others are blindfolded?" Haller asked, not pressing the man.

Fahnestock nodded. "People—at my table," he managed to say.

"Are you telling us all the hostages are blindfolded?" Quist broke in. He had a vision of Lydia, her eyes covered by tape. It shook him.

"I—I think so," Fahnestock managed to say.

Haller looked angry for a moment. "Would you believe

today's terrorist practically goes to school to learn the techniques?" he asked no one in particular. He glanced at Lieutenant Kreevich. "American hostages in Iran— blindfolded! When they expect to hold them for quite a while they blindfold 'em in order to avoid eye contact."

"What's with 'eye contact'?" Quist asked.

"A man with his eyes covered is a blank to his captor," Kreevich said. "With eyes covered there's no chance of any kind of unspoken communication, or arousing any kind of sympathy in the man with the gun."

Haller nodded. "It's really a protection against the possible weakness of your own people, not the captives. Rule number one: 'Don't let anything turn you soft.'"

"The people they're holding are not the enemy," Kreevich said. "The enemies are on the outside."

"The hostages are just bargaining chips," Haller said, his anger creeping into his voice.

"Bastards!" Quist said.

Vic Lorch came back into the office carrying a metal container of oxygen. He helped Fahnestock fit a breathing mask over his face. After a minute or two of inhaling and exhaling Fahnestock removed the mask. Color had come back into his face.

"Thanks for that," he said. "Oh, brother!"

"Tell us what you can, Mr. Fahnestock," Haller said.

"I had dinner there with friends," the little lawyer said, without effort now. "George Miller, one of my law partners, and Milly and Charles Bruno, clients of ours."

Haller wrote down the names. It was a meager beginning of a list of the hostages. Lydia Morton had been the first name on that list.

Fahnestock glanced at Sally Craven. "We'd heard the girl singer was very good. And you are, Miss Craven."

"Thanks," the girl said. It was a whisper.

"Suddenly these people stormed in, waving guns, shouting orders. There was one, sometimes two of them, for every table."

"There are forty-six tables set up for four each, some of them put together for larger parties," Romano said.

"Which means we're talking about more than fifty people with guns," Haller said.

"At least that many," Fahnestock said, "Whites, blacks, a lot of teen-agers. They all wore ski masks. Like people from another world!" He reached for the oxygen mask and used it again. "They told us to stay put, not to move. They had those strips of tape ready and began blindfolding people. I was the first at our table so I didn't see much after the first couple of minutes. People were screaming and yelling, and the gunmen shouting orders."

"Did they manhandle you?" Quist asked, thinking of Lydia.

"Hell, I didn't resist!" Fahnestock said. "I don't know about others. It sounded as if some of the men might have tried something. Maybe they got pushed around. But things quieted down fairly quickly. Then someone shouted for everyone to be still, and this smooth voice told us what the score was. They were asking for Judge Padgett and Carl Zorn to be delivered to them. It was going to take some time for people outside to come through, hours, maybe days. If we behaved ourselves, we would be fed, taken in relays to the rest rooms. If we made trouble we'd be dealt with accordingly."

"You didn't see this smooth-voiced man?"

"No. He came in after my eyes had been taped over." Fahnestock shook his head, a sort of helpless movement. "When I get into a situation where there's any sort of tension or stress my—my breathing starts to act up. I—I guess, after a while, I was doubled over, gasping. My heart was pounding. George Miller started shouing out that I was sick, needed help. This—this smooth voice came to our table. He—he actually took my pulse. He asked me if I had heart trouble. I couldn't answer—couldn't speak. I guess my pulse convinced him. 'I'm going to send you out where you can get medical help,' he said. 'Tell them on the outside that's it's one of my rare kindly moments,' he said. I guess they got in touch with you, and then someone led me out."

"Do you happen to know either Judge Padgett or Carl Zorn?" Haller asked.

"Just by reputation," Fahnestock said. "I'm not in criminal law. What's going to happen? They won't give themselves up to these Reapers, obviously."

"We try to make a deal," Haller said.

"And if they won't deal?"

"We go in!" Quist said in a harsh voice.

"We're a long way from that, Mr. Fahnestock," Haller said.

A state trooper had come in from the outside and was standing in the doorway near to Quist, waiting for Haller to finish his questioning of the lawyer.

"Mr. Orso wants to talk to you, Captain," he said when Haller noticed him.

"Mr. Orso?"

"Mr. Luigi Orso," the trooper said.

"Tell Lefty Orso some other time," Haller said.

There was suddenly a man standing next to the trooper, dark-skinned from much sunshine, wearing a well-tailored three-piece, tropical worsted suit and a pale gray, summer-weight hat with the brim pulled down over very black, very bright eyes.

"Now, Haller," Lefty Luigi Orso said.

Quist knew him by sight from dozens of newspaper photographs and film clips on television—underworld

33

crime boss or Syndicate, if there was such a thing. He had managed to maneuver his way out of a dozen indictments for violence of one sort or another. He was short, square, as powerful-looking as his reputation made him out to be. Looking around the ring of faces, his eyes fastened on Lieutenant Kreevich.

"So we meet again, Kreevich," he said. "What have you got to do with this mess? There's no one dead yet—or is there?"

"Busman's holiday, Lefty," Kreevich said. "The Complex is out of my jurisdiction."

Quist remembered that Kreevich had tried to nail Orso on a murder charge a couple of years back and the gangster had wriggled off the hook.

Orso turned his attention to Haller again. "I got people there in the Cup," he said.

"So do other people here in this room," Haller said.

"So what are you doing about it?" Orso asked.

"I don't have to answer questions from you, Orso," Haller said.

"You don't have to, but I think you ought to think about it," Orso said. "Because if I don't like how you're handling it I'll be taking the whole effing place apart. You started negotiating?"

Haller turned to the state trooper. "Take this character out of here," he said.

The trooper looked shocked. He didn't move.

"The television tells me they won't talk to you till tomorrow morning. You're supposed to tell them then when you'll deliver the judge and the lawyer to them, right?"

"Nobody's going to deliver the judge and the lawyer to them, Lefty," Kreevich said. "You know that."

"Then how do the people in there get out? They've told

you they're going to start sending out dead ones when you don't produce."

"One sure way not to get them out is for you to try to strong-arm the situation, Lefty," Kreevich said.

Orso's tight lips moved in a mirthless smile. "I won't try to go in," he said. "But if you can't make a deal with them in the morning I'll make the deal."

"You?" Haller said.

"I know these crazy freaks," Orso said. "They're not going to buy your lollipops, Haller. If you don't deliver the judge and the counselor, I will. One way or another—I will."

Orso turned and walked out of the office.

3 Someone had brought a counter-sized coffee urn into the office. Quist poured himself a mug and stepped out into the night once again. The raised voices, the tobacco smoke, the sense that no one was following any clear direction, seemed unendurable to him. Everyone had a different idea of what kind of action should be tried. Hostage-taking seemed to be a part of our way of life; most of the people in Garvey's office seemed to have had some kind of indirect contact with that kind of situation. They had to tell how *their* case had been handled. Captain Haller seemed to be willing to listen, patiently, although he must have been through every variation there was. What the hell, Quist thought, Hostage Negotiating Team told the whole story. It was so commonplace that there was a department to handle it. But Lydia was in there! They were three hundred and twenty-six other people, faceless, plus the terrorists. But they didn't

matter to Quist. Only Lydia mattered. How to get her away safely was all he could focus on now. The coffee tasted bitter.

"You have to think about more than Lydia, chum," Kreevich's voice came from behind him. The lieutenant had come out into the night behind his friend.

"Tell me how!" Quist said. Off to the east there was a faint light in the sky. Fifty yards down the path from the office searchlights focused on the mob of reporters held in check by the troopers and security people. Like the people inside, they seemed all to be talking at once. A portable radio blared whatever news was coming from the studios.

"Haller knows his stuff," Kreevich said.

"Orso meant he was going to deliver the judge and Zorn to the Reapers, dead or alive, didn't he?"

"The judge and Zorn will be protected," Kreevich said. "But what I said is fact, Julian. You can't just think about Lydia. Try to get one person out and fail, and you could cost the lives of God knows how many more. Perhaps all of them. There's a man sitting with his hand on a plunger in there who can wipe out the whole place in ten seconds."

"What would Lydia think if she knew I was just standing out here, drinking this lousy coffee, for God's sake?"

"I suspect she thinks you will be playing it cool, listening to people with experience, not thinking like a hysterical kid."

"She's all that matters to me in the whole damned world!"

"Then use your head and what special talents you have to help her."

Quist turned. "How? What special talents?"

Kreevich's lighter flame illuminated his grim face as he got a cigarette going. "Nothing is going to happen, Julian, for hours, maybe days. Haller will negotiate when he can.

That will take time. He'll propose alternatives to their demands. They'll have back and forth at each other. Meanwhile, Haller will prepare for all the possibilities."

"And when we don't deliver, the Voice promises to begin sending out dead bodies. Suppose one of them is Lydia?"

"Let's not call him 'the Voice,'" Kreevich said. "That's a little melodramatic for my taste. Smith is the name he chose. Smith knows who Lydia is. He says he was sitting at the next table to you. You recall him?"

"I wasn't paying attention to anyone but Lydia."

"Smith knows you have contacts with important people all over the area," Kreevich said. "Don't worry about Lydia until he asks you for something you can't or won't do. He won't use her until he has to."

"Whatever he asks me to do I'll do," Quist said.

"Let me tell you what I know about the Reapers," Kreevich said. "It's not enough, but it's a start." He took a deep drag on his cigarette. "It began with a black preacher named Simeon Taylor, back in the sixties. Taylor was an evangelical fanatic, claimed he could cure the sick, heal the crippled. He was for the emancipation of blacks, against the war in Vietnam. Plenty of people, black and white, followed those causes. But the key to his preaching was that all men should be prepared to die for justice. His main targets were the courts, the police, the FBI. Where he felt there had been an injustice his people moved in, gave up their lives if necessary to punish the people responsible. 'Sow death, reap death.' Young people in the sixties bought it by the yard. There have been a couple of dozen bloody revenges over the years. Simeon Taylor was killed— beheaded and left to die on a roadside in a southern town by who knows?—just angry men, the Klan? There has never been any answer. The Reapers had several thousand followers by then, but who runs the show now nobody knows. Names like Smith, Jones, Brown—obviously not real names. Taking hostages has been the pattern in the last few years."

"What became of the hostages?"

"Their demands," Kreevich said, avoiding a direct answer, "have always been for an exchange of people. Once, before Simeon Taylor died, someone gave in to those demands—turned over three men in exchange for a couple of dozen hostages. Those three men were mutilated, left hanging from trees on the outskirts of the town where it happened. No one capitulated again. There have been three occasions since then when they destroyed not only the hostages but themselves."

"Then they'll do what they say," Quist said.

"That's the record."

"Then we have no way to go except to break in and hope we don't get blown up ourselves," Quist said, his voice unsteady. "Someone might survive that. Lydia might be a survivor."

"You like the odds?" Kreevich asked.

"So we just sit and wait for the slaughter?" Quist cried out.

"Easy does it, chum," Kreevich said, quietly. "The people in there with Smith have to believe in him, have to believe in what old Simeon Taylor preached. Haller is right, you know. There may be a way to create doubts among them. There has to be a way to make the man, or men, who sit by that detonator hesitate about pushing down the plunger that will blow the place, and themselves, to glory. If there is a way to start them wondering, arguing among themselves, we have a chance."

"And how do we do that?"

Kreevich gave his friend a thin smile. "I talked about your special talents, Julian. Selling people on a product, a cause, an entertainment, is your business. You, and

Garvey, and Lydia, and the rest of the people in your office are geniuses at that kind of selling. The survival of three hundred and twenty-seven people may depend on your being able to sell fifty-odd fanatics that their leadership is dishonest, using them for their own gains, laughing behind their backs at Simeon Taylor's cause. 'Sow dissent, reap freedom.'"

"And how do we do that?"

"Sit down and *think!*" Kreevich said sharply. "Stop wondering how you can jump through a window and save a single lady. There are probably going to be days before we come to the crisis. Who is Smith? Where is his bank account? Who is jealous of his power, a Judas who may help? Carl Zorn may be able to help when we get to him. Judge Padgett may know things that will be useful. I suggest that you stop hanging around here and use the time we've got to find people to talk to, people who know more than the police records will show us. I think I can persuade Haller that you may be the best man in the world to talk to, to listen, to come up with some kind of useful way to work."

"You want me to leave here, with Lydia shut away in the Cup—with adhesive tape over her eyes, with Smith at her side?"

"You want her out, don't you?"

"Oh God, Mark!"

"Let us handle it here," Kreevich said. "If there is any reason to believe that going in is the answer, let trained cops and security people do the job. You're not a two-gun tough guy, Julian. You're a thinker, a planner. Use what you've got, and let us use what we've got. We have the muscle, you use your head."

Quist was silent for a moment. The strip of light was widening in the east. Dawn was creeping in on them.

"The hostage situation in Iran went on for months," Kreevich said, "while the Shah played croquet on the lawn of his rented palace in Egypt. There was no substitute for him to buy those hostages their freedom. Only Judge Padgett and Carl Zorn will satisfy the people here in the Cup. They'll wait. They'll wait for quite a while, Julian. We have to believe we have time to make a plan, a reasonable amount of time."

A state trooper was coming up the path toward them from the area where the reporters were contained. He spotted Kreevich.

"Lieutenant? There's a woman down there looking for Mr. Quist."

"I'm Quist," Quist said.

"I know, sir. This woman has clothes for you."

"Has what?"

"Clothes. She says she's your secretary. A Miss Parmalee?"

"Connie, for God's sake," Quist said.

"Shall we let her come up?" the trooper asked. "We've been through her suitcase. It is just clothes, men's clothes."

Connie Parmalee had been Quist's private secretary for a number of years, a tall girl with copper-colored hair, her eyes always hidden behind tinted granny glasses, a sensational long-legged figure. A very mod girl for a very mod establishment. She had only one old-fashioned failing. She was a secretary in love with her boss. The problem was that between Connie and the fulfillment of any dreams she might have was Lydia. There wasn't even the satisfaction of telling herself that Lydia was a bitch whose bitchiness would eventually turn Quist off. Lydia wasn't a bitch. She was a delightful woman, witty, compassionate, highly skillful at her job as a writer and researcher for Julian Quist Associates. She could probably, Connie told herself, make her look like an amateur in bed. There was no way you could outdo Lydia with Quist, and there was no way you could resent her because of it. Dan Garvey, who played the female field, had devoted himself to Connie for a stretch of time, and Connie had played his game because she couldn't play the game she dreamed of playing. "Connie Come Lately" Garvey called her. "You came on the scene too late for Julian or you might have landed him. I'm sorry for you for that. But I can't go on making love to a girl who is always wishing I was someone else. It's bad for the ego."

She came up the path, carrying a suitcase.

"I thought you'd want to change out of your evening clothes," she said. "You had these things at the office."

"You're wonderful," Quist said. "I was beginning to feel like an idiot in this suit."

"Lydia?" she asked.

"We don't know how anybody is in there," Quist said. "You know Mark Kreevich."

"Hello, Lieutenant," she said. "Is there anything I can do for you, Julian?"

"Stick around while I change," Quist said. "We're just beginning to try to make plans." He took the suitcase and went back into the office complex with it.

"How bad is it, Lieutenant?" she asked, watching Quist go.

"Bad," Kreevich said. "Not hopeless yet, but bad."

"Is there anything I can do?"

"Help to keep him from going off his rocker," Kreevich said. "Let me tell you how it is."

Radio and television reporters, crowding outside the barriers set up by security, were in some ways a pain in the neck to Captain Haller, Vic Lorch, and Captain Jansen, in charge of the state police detail. These people, along with the newspaper reporters, had to be covered almost as closely as the terrorists in the Cup. Someone overzealous could endanger the whole process of negotiation, if there was to be any that really counted. But they had produced some positive results for the men in charge. Constant reports on radio and television all over the eastern part of the United States, almost from the moment that the terrorists had taken over the Cup and the hostages, had alerted people who might be useful. Clogged telephone lines had kept some of them from getting through, but finally, when lines were cleared for police use, offers of help began to be heard.

One of the very first people to contact the police was Judge Stephen Padgett. He owned an old brownstone in the Murray Hill section of Manhattan and lived there, attended by a couple named Jason and Sarah Brinker. The judge had been widowed some years ago.

"What can I do to be of use?" Judge Padgett asked Haller when he was able to get through.

"Stay put," Haller told him. "We're redoubling the guard outside your house. The greatest danger for you at the moment, Judge, is not the Reapers, but Luigi Orso."

"What has Orso got to do with this?" Padgett asked.

"Friends of his are among the hostages. If we don't turn you and Zorn over to the Reapers, he threatens to do it himself."

"Shouldn't I get out of here?" Padgett asked. "Everybody knows where I live."

"Not till we can arrange for a place we can protect without any loopholes. Look out your windows and you'll see a small fleet of police cars out there now. I know you can't live that way forever, Your Honor, but we need time to arrange a change for you—and for so damn many other things."

"I think I understand," the judge said. "I'm here alone with the couple who look out for me, you know."

"Someone in authority will be there to talk to you very quickly. It may not be a policeman, but he will be working

42

for us and will be brought to you by police. Do you have files there in the house on the Reapers, Your Honor?"

"My office."

"Can someone bring them there to you?"

"After eight-thirty, when the office building opens and I can send one of my law clerks there."

"Do that, please," Haller said. "One other thing, Judge Padgett. Do you know where Carl Zorn can be located? We haven't been able to find him."

"We aren't close friends, you know," the judge said. "I don't keep tabs on him. He has an apartment here in town."

"Not there," Haller said.

"Aren't you cops guarding him?"

"A little too loosely, I guess. Our man doesn't report every hour on the hour—unless there's trouble."

"Sorry I can't help," Judge Padgett said. "I'll be waiting for someone to show up here."

Captain Jansen, the state trooper, asked about the protection setups for Judge Padgett and Carl Zorn. "I hadn't heard anything about it till someone caught me up on it when I got here tonight," he said to Haller.

"Paul Kramer was near the top in the hierarchy that runs the Reapers. He was charged and convicted of the murder of a federal prosecutor who had won a case against a group of the Reapers in the South. 'Sow death, reap death.' Zorn was appointed by the attorney general to handle the case against Kramer. Judge Padgett presided. There were all kinds of wild threats against those two during the trial. They were carefully guarded. Zorn won the case and Kramer was sentenced to life. There were appeals. Oh, they've got lawyers, these people. Good ones. The state supreme court denied an appeal. The United States Supreme Court refused to hear the case. That all took months. Kramer was sent to Attica to begin serving his time. About three weeks ago he managed to hang himself in his cell. A Reaper fails in what he sets out to do, he takes his own life. Name of the game. In the months during the appeals the protection against Padgett and Zorn was relaxed, but after Kramer's suicide it was renewed. Threats had started up again. The Reapers evidently decided they were too tough to get at in a simple hit. So this!"

"Or they want to tell the world that you can't attack the Reapers without paying for it in spades," Kreevich said. He was standing in the corner of Garvey's office with Quist, who had changed into the summer tweed jacket, slacks, and a navy blue turtleneck sports shirt Connie had brought him.

"Then the cops guarding Zorn know where he is," Jansen said.

"But wherever they are they haven't heard yet what's happened here," Kreevich said.

Haller nodded. "They'll be in touch when they do," he said. "Not everyone in the world is listening to the radio or watching television at five o'clock in the morning."

"What about Lefty Orso?" Jansen asked.

Haller looked grim. "Problem there is who to cover," he said. "Orso doesn't do his own dirty work. But he's got an army of goons to call on."

"You say Kramer had a good lawyer," Quist said.

"Martin Wilshire, 'the great defender,'" Kreevich said. "Sonofabitch has made a fortune defending mobsters, Syndicate killers, crooked politicians."

"And must know all there is to know about the Reapers," Quist said.

"Let's get down to brass tacks, Mr. Quist," Haller said. "Kreevich has told me you're willing to help."

"As against just standing around and going quietly crazy," Quist said.

"Your Miss Morton is at the top of the news," Haller

said. "She was the first hostage we identified and the reporters have it. It's not going to surprise anyone that you'd do everything possible to get her free. You wouldn't necessarily be working for us. It won't surprise anyone if you're circulating, asking questions. I'd like to turn you loose on Judge Padgett, and Zorn when we locate him. They may talk more freely to a man with your problem than to the police."

"Let's face it," Kreevich said. "A desperate man, like Julian, might do more to break the deadlock here than cops who will play strictly by the rules."

"But you've got to play by the rules, Mr. Quist," Haller said.

"They won't know that," Quist said in a flat, cold voice. "I have a question for you, Captain."

"Fire away."

"When Smith first talked to us on that phone, he knew exactly who was in this room—Broadhurst, Coleman, Fairchild, Dan Garvey, Vic Lorch, me. He knew later when you'd joined the party, Captain. That can only mean there's someone outside the Cup keeping him informed. That person can't be a stranger to us or we'd spot him at once. So—a trooper, one of Vic's security people, a reporter, someone who works here at maintenance or in the stables at the track, someone whose presence here is perfectly natural at the moment. Someone, for Christ's sake, in this room right now."

There was an uncomfortable silence as people looked around at each other. In addition to the cops and Vic Lorch, there were the two girls, Sally Craven and Connie Parmalee; Mike Romano, the manager of the Cup who had been sent out by Smith to warn them; Fahnestock, the emphysema victim; the three trustees; two of Lorch's men.

"If Smith's man is here now, there's no point in my trying anything," Quist said. "Smith will be forewarned."

"I think it's a chance you have to take—if you're willing," Haller said after a long silence.

"What choice do I have?" Quist asked. "But I promise, if it's someone in this room and anything happens to Lydia and the other hostages, you'll have a murder on your hands, so help me God!"

"Feel better?" Kreevich asked. "Big man, big threats!"

He and Quist and Connie Parmalee were standing by Quist's car in the parking lot. It was quite light outside now, a gold glow in the eastern sky. Outdoor searchlights were still focused on the Stirrup Cup, but inside drapes were pulled over the windows. It, somehow, looked cold and hostile. Inside three hundred and twenty-seven people, covered by terrorists' guns, must be straining for some kind of hint about what was being done to help them. Quist guessed that Smith must have told his captives that there would be no action until ten o'clock in the morning. It would be a way to keep them quiet.

On the far side of the Cup, out of sight from the location of Quist's car in the parking lot, a Complex task force had set up a coffee and sandwich counter for the press. Quist and Kreevich and Connie could hear the ever-present radio, but not clearly enough to distinguish words. A death watch, Quist found himself thinking. There would be nothing new for another five hours. Good reporters like Rusty Grimes and Hal Linder and Helen Bates were probably long gone, back in the city trying to get statements from the judge and Carl Zorn, and anyone else who might have information about the Reapers.

"I meant what I said," Quist said. "If someone in that office is selling us out—"

"We'll take care of him," Kreevich said. "Threatening murder may make you feel better, chum, but we need you using your head, putting together what you can find out for us."

"What is it you expect I'll find?" Quist asked.

"Who is Smith? Who is close to him on the outside? Does he have a family, a woman? Is he the head man, the inspirational leader the Reapers will die for if he asks it, or is he just a lieutenant in command of this particular action? If that's the way it is, we're looking for someone higher up, someone who can call off his dogs if we can bring the right kind of pressure to bear. What we've got inside the Cup is someone who calls himself Smith, an obviously phony name, and an army of creeps in ski masks. Haller can't negotiate effectively unless he knows who he's talking to. He needs to know something about Smith, about the real person in command if he isn't Smith. He needs to be able to let Smith know, when he talks to him five hours from now, that he isn't confronting a zero. He needs to be able to drop the names of Smith's wife, his kids if he's got any, his woman or women, if that's the way it is, his headquarters, his bank account. Any real knowledge about any of those things will give Haller just a little more edge than he's got now."

"You mentioned a bank account back in the office," Quist said.

"I'm a cynic," Kreevich said. "I don't believe in faith healers. I don't believe in causes like doing God's work by terrorizing innocent people, or mutilating victims and hanging them from trees!" The lieutenant's own anger was clear in his voice. "Someone at the top is getting rich by using these crackpot fanatics to spread his particular brand of violence. You want to look at my crystal ball?"

"Show it to me, Mark."

"Before this day is out someone will 'escape' from the Cup. I put quotation marks around that word *escape*. It could be Broadhurst's wife, it could be one of Orso's friends. The escape will have been paid for. The money will go into someone's pocket—Smith's, the Great White Father's? The person who escapes may not know it, and the person who pays won't open his mouth about it."

"Then the whole thing is a fraud, a kidnapping for money?"

"Not quite. I wish it was. We could negotiate, we could deal if it was just money. The Reapers, the little people in the ski masks, have got to believe in the Cause. 'Sow death, reap death!' Justice by the sword! The organization would fall apart if they knew someone was getting rich off what they're doing. But somewhere there's a healthy bank account. In whose name? Is it in Switzerland with just a number attached to it? Is it spread out in dozens of small accounts? I don't think we're going to find those answers in a hurry, Julian. We can't begin to look until we know who Smith is, or who the Great White Father is, if he isn't Smith."

"It's hard to believe," Quist said.

"Let me ask you a hypothetical question," Kreevich said. "You are going back to the city. Someone calls you in your office. Lydia will be allowed to escape—for a price. And silence, of course. They'll know how much to ask for, because they'll know how much money you can lay hands on. Would you pay to get Lydia free?"

The two men stared at each other for a moment.

"God help me, I guess I would," Quist said.

"And never tell a soul as long as you live," Kreevich said. "I wouldn't blame you. In your shoes I'd do the same thing. It's a very profitable sideline, wouldn't you say?"

"I'm wasting time," Quist said.

"When you get to Padgett's house, there'll be a Sergeant Kaminski there. He knows you. You've met him in my office. He'll get you in to the judge. Good luck. I'll call you there in about an hour. We may have located Carl Zorn by then."

"Thanks, Mark."

"You see the motorcycle cop over there by the exit?"

Quist looked across the parking lot. A cop on a motorcycle raised his arm in a gesture of recognition.

"Don't spare the horses, chum," Kreevich said. "Officer Callahan will lead you into town, see to it you're not picked up for speeding."

Quist had driven the expressway out to the Complex many times, but never at the speed they covered the trip back into Manhattan that morning. It was, perhaps, a good thing. Concentration on driving, following Officer Callahan on his siren-shrieking motorcycle, made thinking about Lydia, the problems that lay ahead, impossible. He was almost not aware of Connie Parmalee who sat beside him, gripping the window ledge on her side so tightly her knuckles were white marbles.

There wasn't much traffic on the city streets and Callahan raced them across town to the brownstone where Judge Padgett lived. Quist pulled up and stopped. Callahan grinned at him.

"Paul Newman could use you on his race-driving team," he said.

Quist took his hands off the wheel, not quite sure they'd come away. "Remind me not to suggest we try it again," he said. "Thanks."

There were five or six police cars parked in the block, cops everywhere. Sergeant Kaminski, a dark, square man in plain clothes, came over to the car.

"Morning, Mr. Quist," he said. "You made good time. The judge is expecting you."

Quist glanced at his watch. It was a quarter to six. Just a little more than four hours before Haller would be talking to Smith.

"I'll be here when you're ready to go back," Callahan told Quist, grinning at him.

"I—I'll wait for you here," Connie said in a small voice.

Quist looked at her. What a good girl, he thought.

"Come in with me," he said. "I may need you to take notes—if you're up to it."

"I may never be up to anything again," she said. "Do you know you almost hit a hundred miles an hour at one stretch out there?"

"The speedometer lies," Quist said. "That's how they sell these cars."

Kaminski led them to the door of the house. Two cops, holstered guns at the ready, stood in the vestibule. "This is Julian Quist, and his secretary," the sergeant told them.

One of the cops rang the doorbell. The door was promptly opened by a tall man wearing a white housecoat.

"I'm Jason Brinker, Mr. Quist," he said. "The judge is expecting you. If you'll come with me, please."

It was a lived-in house, warm and friendly. Brinker led the way through an entrance hall to what was obviously the dining room. There was a mahogany sideboard with a handsome silver tea service on it. Judge Stephen Padgett sat at a round table, a silver coffeepot and silver cream pitcher and a sugar bowl with silver tongs slipped through a loop at the top of the handle, surrounding a china coffee cup. As Quist came in he put down a pipe he'd been smoking in a silver ashtray and stood up. Quist introduced Connie.

"Please sit down, both of you," the judge said. "Is it possible you'd like to freshen up, either or both of you?"

He was the perfect picture of a judge, Quist thought: white hair, keen gray eyes, a face lined by experience, a rich voice that could have belonged to an actor—or a judge.

Connie indicated that she'd like to "freshen up." A woman wearing a black, uniform-type dress and a white apron had come through a swinging door from the kitchen pantry.

"Mrs. Brinker will take care of you, Miss Parmalee," the judge said. "Can I offer you both some breakfast? I had mine quite a while ago. I've been up most of the night."

"Coffee would be fine for both of us, I think," Quist said.

Connie went off with Mrs. Brinker. Quist sat down at the table and Brinker went to the pantry for cups.

"From what I've heard it's been a rough night for you, Mr. Quist," the judge said.

"Rough," Quist said. He closed his eyes tight for a moment. They were still stinging from the tensions of the drive in. "There's nothing new to tell you, Judge, if you've been listening to the radio. The Reapers took over the Stirrup Cup just before midnight. I'd gone to a business meeting in an adjoining building, leaving Miss Morton, one of my partners and my—my—"

"Your woman, I take it," the judge said.

"The dearest person in the world to me, Your Honor, not just a woman."

"I understand."

"We are four hours from what I hope will only be our first deadline, Judge. Captain Haller, negotiator for the police, will be talking to a man who calls himself Smith and who appears to be in command of the terrorists inside the Cup. Haller needs ammunition. You and Carl Zorn may be able to provide him with some. That's why I'm here. Undercover cops are combing the city for any leads that will take them into the center of the design that is the Reapers. Now I know your files on the Kramer case will not be available for a while, maybe three hours, but Haller can't wait that long for any kind of clue."

"My files will be available in a very few minutes," the judge said. "Your Lieutenant Kreevich, who appears to be an efficient officer, has arranged to get my office building and my private office opened. I routed one of my law clerks out of bed and he's at the office, identifying the Kramer files, and will bring them here at once. I thought it might be he when you people rang the front doorbell."

"Haller will be grateful," Quist said.

"If there is anything in the files of use," the judge said.

"Weeks of notes on the trial? There's bound to be useful information."

"You think so?" The judge gave Quist a bitter little smile. "Reams of notes made on objections to rulings of mine made by Martin Wilshire, Kramer's lawyer. Those objections were the basis for an appeal. My files, I'm afraid, cover legal points, not personal matters that would be helpful to your Captain Haller."

"What Haller needs is to know whether Smith, the man in charge at the Cup, is the Great White Father, the Mahatma, the Ayatollah of the Reapers, or just a soldier in charge of an action," Quist said.

"Zorn was trying to find the same answers in the case of Paul Kramer," the judge said. "Was he the head man, or just a mercenary?"

"And the answer?"

"I don't think Zorn ever came up with an answer," the judge said. "There is, however, a fact to bear in mind, Mr. Quist. After Kramer was tried, convicted, held in custody while appeals were heard, the Reapers went right on with their pattern of violence. Kramer hanged himself at Attica three weeks ago, so someone else is giving the orders for what's going on out at the Stirrup Cup. Kramer isn't, at least, today's White Father. My guess is your Mr. Smith isn't either. He's contained out there by the police. He knew he would be. I have a feeling that the man at the top doesn't walk into any self-made traps."

"So you don't think Smith is the head man?"

"In the beginning," the judge said, "when the Reapers were founded by Simeon Taylor, he was always visible. He was the healer, the founder of the faith. When he was murdered by the Klan—I've always thought it was the Klan—whoever took over from Taylor has remained invisible. Your man Smith is visible, so I assume he isn't it."

"But there are people who know," Quist said.

"Of course." The judge allowed Brinker to pour the fresh coffee that he had brought from the kitchen. "There is one man who almost certainly knows."

"Carl Zorn?"

The judge shook his head. "Martin Wilshire, the lawyer," the judge said. "He's handled three or four cases for indicted Reapers. But he won't talk. Lawyer-client confidentiality."

"He won't talk to save three hundred and twenty-seven people?"

The judge's laugh was mirthless. "You want to guess what his fees are for handling cases for the Reapers? It's perfectly legal for a lawyer to defend guilty clients, and it's perfectly ethical for him to keep private conversations private."

"Heat applied to him?"

"I wish you luck," the judge said. "He's a tough cookie." He shifted uncomfortably in his chair. Quist noticed he hadn't touched the fresh coffee Brinker had brought. He tried relighting his pipe, but the minute he had it going he put it down again as if the smoke tasted bad. "Smith is a name that came up during Kramer's trial," he said. "Not from the defense, Wilshire and the Reapers, but from a street cop who was a witness for Zorn and the prosecution.

53

That cop had been on the trail you're following too. Who is the head man? He thought at first it was someone named Smith, but then he learned that what you might call cliché names, like Smith, Jones, and Brown, were used by a lot of different people, like a rank—sergeant, lieutenant, captain. Smith just meant you were a key figure."

"Like King of the Hill?" Quist asked.

"Possibly. But, understand, Mr. Quist, what I'm trying to say is that the man who is called Smith today may not be the same man who is called Smith tomorrow. It's a title. The man in charge of what's going on at the Stirrup Cup is called Smith. The man who is what you call King of the Hill, the head Reaper, may also be called Smith. Not the same man."

"But Wilshire and Zorn might be able to put real names to people?"

"Wilshire, certainly; Zorn only maybe. If Zorn knows, he didn't find out till after Kramer's trial. He could have used your King of the Hill as a prosecution witness if he could have named him at the time."

"And you don't think your files will help us?"

"Naming the head man was vital during Kramer's trial," the judge said. "No name ever surfaced. Kramer was buttoned up tight, wouldn't tell the cops or Zorn anything. Clever interrogation on the witness stand never produced a slip. Detectives who worked on the case before it came to trial never came up with any key names. Oh, there were hundreds of names of members of the Reapers, strong-arm kids, praying women, street-corner orators. But not key names, not leader names. The murder of Simeon Taylor had long since driven those key people underground."

"If Miss Parmalee could go through your files," Quist said, "she might just come across something." Connie had come back into the room.

The judge shook his head. "She's welcome, you're

welcome," he said. "But you'll only find legal notes, comments on objections Wilshire made to my rulings. Not what you're looking for, I'm afraid. However, Mr. Quist—"

"Yes?"

"I'm aware of your personal distress, your lady a prisoner. But I have problems, too, Mr. Quist. You see," and the judge's smile was twisted, "I enjoy being alive."

"Of course you do, sir," Quist said.

"You're not young enough to have to 'sir' me, Mr. Quist. It has a nice, polite ring to it, though. Almost disappeared from today's world, that kind of courtesy. Today's world is a damned scary place to live in."

"That's for sure," Quist said.

"Just give me a few minutes, Mr. Quist. I know time is important to you. You need something you can use to negotiate with these terrorists. You need some kind of weapon to save several hundred people, and, in particular, your own lady. You want her alive, and well, and unharmed. Well, I, too, want to be alive, and well, and unharmed. What is your Lieutenant Kreevich going to do to protect me? Oh, I know this house is surrounded by cops, uniformed and in street clothes. I will be safe, I suppose, as long as they can afford an army to protect me. But what about tomorrow, or next week, or next month? Tell me, is there any secret talk about turning me and Carl Zorn over to the Reapers?"

"None at all, Judge. It is taken for granted that's an impossibility."

"What about Orso and his gangsters? Has it occurred to you that all Orso has to do is place some sharpshooters where he can get a shot at me—and at Carl Zorn? If Zorn and I are dead, your man Smith has no use for his hostages anymore, does he? The hostages, including Orso's friends, will be released and the terrorists allowed to go free, since they won't have harmed anybody. It would be a simple way out of the dilemma for everyone, wouldn't it? Everyone except Zorn and me."

"What are you asking me, Judge?"

"How can we be kept safe?" Judge Padgett asked, his voice unsteady. "There are several thousand Reapers circulating around the country. I don't know who they are, you don't know who they are. There are probably a hundred gunmen on Orso's payroll. Nobody knows who they are, either. How can we be protected against people without any faces?"

"Nobody is going to get at you in this house, Mr. Stephen." It was Jason Brinker, the houseman, who spoke. He was standing by the sideboard, waiting to bring fresh coffee.

"I appreciate your dedication and devotion, Jason," the judge said. "But to stay locked in this house forever is not living!"

"I can't answer your question, Judge," Quist said. "But I think I can project something for you. In a little more than three hours Captain Haller will be talking to Smith. He isn't going to have you or Zorn to deliver. He's going to play for time. He thinks he will get it. Smith indicated in his conversation with Haller that they could hold out in the Cup for several days, if necessary. They seem prepared for that. That's time of sorts. Orso, I think, won't move until he's convinced the negotiations are breaking down. That, too, is time. I'll take your question to Kreevich and Haller and the others and they may have answers for you. But I think you'll be safe for a while, unless somebody triggers a holocaust."

The judge leaned back in his chair, pressing the tips of his fingers against his eyes for a moment. "If you were in my place, Mr. Quist," he said finally, "approaching seventy years of age, your professional career at an end, your woman gone—as my dear wife is gone—with no real future except to sit in the garden and let the sun warm you, would you, in that position, drive out to the Stirrup Cup and give yourself up to Smith in order to free the hostages?"

"Taking Carl Zorn with you?" Quist asked.

The judge actually laughed. "You would laugh, too, if you knew Zorn, Mr. Quist. He would never in this world give himself up for someone else, not even for his own mother!"

"You want an honest answer, don't you?" Quist asked.

"As honest as you can make it," the judge said.

"If I was told that if I walked into the Cup, Lydia would be set free, unharmed, I might go in," Quist said. "My life for hers, I probably would. But to save three hundred and twenty-six strangers, I don't know. If the purpose was to punish me for a legal and justifiable action, I would have to give it a hell of a lot of thought. And so that you don't waste your time thinking, Judge Padgett, let me say that I don't believe the Reapers will be satisfied with just one of you. They want you *and* Zorn, probably Zorn more than you. He presented the case that convinced a jury to convict Kramer. You only passed sentence after the fact. No, Your Honor, I don't think, if I were you, I'd just walk in and give myself up. I don't think it would free the hostages or end the terror."

"Thank you for your honest opinion," the judge said. "I think I hear my clerk in the outer hall. That means my files are here. If you and Miss Parmalee want to go through them, you're welcome. Fred Watson, my clerk, will help in any way he can."

"One question for you, Your Honor," Quist said. "Is there any doubt in your mind that Paul Kramer was guilty of murdering a federal prosecutor? You presided at the trial."

"No doubt whatever," the judge said promptly. "I don't think the Reapers themselves would deny that Kramer killed a man. But their faith, their cult, tells them he was justified. That same cult tells them that we were not justified in punishing him. We, they believe, must pay the price for that."

"No one has suggested there is a way you could buy yourself out of this, Judge?"

The judge looked surprised. "Buy my way out? I don't follow."

"Lieutenant Kreevich thinks that behind all the Reapers' mumbo jumbo about 'Sow death, reap death,' someone has found a way to build up a massive bank account somewhere."

The judge stood up and held out his hand. "You've made me feel better, Mr. Quist. It makes me feel better to know that someone else thinks as I have thought for a long time. There is a get-rich-quick aspect to the Reapers' operation, and I've always been sure of it. It's a relief to know that someone who may be concerned for my survival is looking down the same tunnel for the same light that I am. Good luck; and if you can keep me posted I'd appreciate it."

4

On the desk in Dan Garvey's office, which had been turned into a headquarters for the police at the Complex, was an electric clock. The second hand moved in a steady, rhythmic beat, like a healthy heart, toward ten o'clock. D day, the hour of the first decisions.

Outside, daylight had transformed the area into something more nearly like normal. The Stirrup Cup was always closed in the mornings, blinds drawn over the windows. Except for the army of news people gathered around their improvised coffee stand, and the uniformed troopers and security men in plain clothes patrolling all sides of the Cup, the normal activities went on. Trucks brought loads of hay and grain to the Shed Row area of the racetrack. Horses had to be fed and cared for, hostages or no hostages. Exercise boys had some of the animals out on the track, a daily routine. Other trucks brought food supplied to the commissary arrangements at the track, at Shed Row, and in the main Complex arena. People had to be fed, too, hostages or no hostages. Clean-up crews, picking up the debris of discarded cigarette packages and candy wrappers, beer bottles and paper cups, an occasional handkerchief or scarf inadvertantly dropped by someone, went about their routine business.

Almost no one went anywhere without constant curious glances at the building where the hostages were held. What was going on behind those drape-covered windows? Were over three hundred people blindfolded as the emphysema victim had suggested? How were they fed? Were they escorted to the rest rooms in groups or individually? Were some of them trying to talk their way out? Was ransom money being offered? Had any of them managed to sleep in the eight hours since their imprisonment had begun? Finally, there was question number one. Who, on the outside, was in contact with Smith on the inside? By now, with the aid of the telephone company, police were monitoring all calls in and out of the Cup. That was academic, because after the first hour when the monitoring system was in effect there had been no calls. No answered calls, at any rate. Only one line into the Cup had been kept in service, the private line to Mike Romano's office on which Haller was to make his ten o'clock call. People trying to reach other phones in the Cup, frantic relatives and friends, were informed by a recorded voice that the number they were trying to reach was out of service. Smith or anyone else inside the Cup could have made an out-call, monitored of course, at any time, but no one tried. Smith must have been quite aware of how closely he was covered. He must have been aware, well in advance, of just how Haller would handle what he called "the containment" of the hostages and their captors.

Haller had cleared Garvey's office of everyone but key people. The rich trustees, complaining bitterly, had been escorted out. Sally Craven, and the emphysema victim, and Mike Romano were gone. With Haller were Lieutenant Kreevich, Captain Jansen of the state police, Dan Garvey, and Vic Lorch, head of Complex security. At eight-thirty the press committee, consisting of Rusty Grimes, Hal Linder, and Helen Bates, was invited in.

"Nothing new," Haller told them.

"What about the judge and Carl Zorn?" Rusty Grimes asked.

"Julian Quist has visited the judge," Haller told him. "Willing to help but nothing very concrete to offer. We have not yet been in touch with Zorn."

"You don't know where he is?"

"Not at this moment."

"Haven't the police been covering him since Kramer's trial?"

"Yes and no," Haller said. "Zorn did not want to be surrounded by cops. He hired his own bodyguards. The higherups agreed to that arrangement, provided Zorn or one of his men would be in touch with headquarters at least once a day. They normally call in around noon."

"Two hours too late," Grimes said.

"Maybe it will give us an extra two hours," Haller said.

"In which to do what?" Grimes asked.

"Get ready for whatever," Haller said in his quiet voice.

"Attack?"

"The final resort," Haller said. "First, at ten o'clock, we try to stall, to deal."

"You think they may finally settle for money?"

"Not openly," Haller said. "Smith's people are fanatics with a cause. The Cause demands the delivery of Judge Padgett and Zorn. If the word got out that someone was taking money, there could be a rebellion."

"So no one will take money."

"But the word can get out that someone has," Dan Garvey said. "It may get to be my job and Julian Quist's to convince them that someone has."

"We may try that when everything else has failed," Haller said. "Confusion and dissent inside before we try a breakin."

"I'd like to ask a question," Helen Bates said. "What is Lieutenant Kreevich doing here? He's Manhattan Homicide. This is not his jurisdiction, his beat."

Kreevich grinned at her. "You object, Helen?"

"It's a question I've been asked by our people on the outside."

"There are dozens of unsolved homicides in Manhattan, Miss Bates," Haller said, "in which the police believe the Reapers were involved. Lieutenant Kreevich is following up on those cases. If this were happening in Timbuktu, he would probably be there."

"But the fact is, Mark, that Julian Quist is your close friend, and Lydia Morton, his girl, who is a hostage, is also your friend. Isn't that really why you're here? At the taxpayers' expense?"

Kreevich's face had gone hard. "It gives me an extra interest," he said. "Since I've had dealings with the Reapers in the past, Captain Haller thinks I can be helpful here. If he hadn't asked me, I'd toss in my badge and be doing what I could at my own expense. Your concern for the taxpayers is touching, ma'am."

"Both Padgett and Zorn are residents of Manhattan. The police there are just as concerned as the police out here," Captain Jansen said.

"Let's get back to what we can do to help," Rusty Grimes said.

"There is one thing," Haller said. "In the first hour, before we got control of the telephones, someone was tipping Smith off to everything that was going on outside. He knew who was in this office. He knew when I arrived. Vic Lorch is covering everyone on the lot here, trying to spot that pigeon. It occurs to me that it just might have been a reporter, promised a scoop if he played footsie with Smith. There are what, a hundred of them out there? Checking out would keep you busy, Rusty."

"That's pretty farfetched," Grimes said.

"The whole damned business is pretty farfetched, Rusty. You asked how you could help."

A state trooper came in the office door and addressed Captain Jansen. "There's a man outside, sir, from Kilgore and Skaggs, the architects who built this building. He's brought blueprints."

"Bring him in," Captain Haller said.

The electric clock kept up its steady beat. A quarter to nine and counting down.

The people in Garvey's office crowded around the flat-topped desk to study the blueprints that the architects' man spread out for them. There were no hoped-for secret or forgotten ways in or out of the Stirrup Cup. It was a new building, without additions that might have created unplanned access routes. The ground floor consisted of the large restaurant area and the adjoining kitchens, Mike Romano's office, rest rooms for both men and women customers. The basement, large and deep, contained a wine cellar, freezing compartments, storage areas for all manner of things, from canned foods to cleaning equipment. There was a utility room that housed heating and air-conditioning equipment and fuse boxes. There was a freight elevator that opened out onto the back platform where the man with emphysema had been released. There was a dumbwaiter going from basement to kitchen. There was the main entrance, used by customers, which opened into a foyer, flanked by a coat room. There were two large doors on each side of the building, used and marked on the plan as "Fire Exits." On the second floor were eight small bedrooms with shower-baths used by some of the permanent kitchen help, and a large open space where extra tables, extra chairs, and equipment replacements of one sort or another were stored. Above that, reached only by a trap door in the ceiling, was an air space, empty.

"I suppose, in the dark, you could cut your way through the roof and come down from the top," the architect suggested.

"Magically noiseless," Haller said, not impressed. "This whole business was carefully planned in advance. They know that building better than we do, even with the plans in front of us."

"I've been wondering, Captain," Dan Garvey said. "The explosives they have planted were obviously in place before the Reapers took over last night. They had to have inside help to manage that, didn't they? It couldn't have been done in business hours with the place fully staffed. Isn't that more evidence that there's someone connected with the Complex, who can come and go without arousing suspicion, who's on the Reapers' payroll?"

"Same person who kept Smith informed about who was where in that first hour," Haller said. He turned to Vic Lorch, the security chief. He didn't ask the question. It was obvious.

"It's hard to get a handle on it," Lorch said. "Everyone we could ask who might have seen something, heard something, is locked up in that goddamned place!"

"Night watchman? Planting stuff there must have been done after hours, mustn't it?"

Lorch was angry. The whole suggestion reflected on his efficiency. "Truckloads of stuff come in here every day," he said. "Boxes and crates unloaded on that rear platform, taken down to the basement on the freight elevator. Could be marked 'canned apricots' or some damn thing. Could have been stored down there for two, three days—a week! Unless somebody needed canned apricots—! When they broke in they knew what to look for and where to find it. People trained to put it in place at the last minute."

"Possible," Haller said. His smile was bitter. "After it's all over we can question the help, right?"

"If they're still alive," Garvey said. Round and round the mulberry bush, he thought.

Nine o'clock in Manhattan.

From a telephone in Judge Padgett's study Quist dialed a number listed in the book for Martin Wilshire, attorney. A brisk, operator-type girl's voice answered.

"Mr. Wilshire will not be in until ten o'clock," she said when Quist asked for the lawyer.

"This is an emergency. Where can I reach him?" Quist asked. "I don't have a home phone listed for him."

"It's an unlisted number. I'm afraid I can't give it to you," the operator said.

"My name is Julian Quist. You undoubtedly can reach Mr. Wilshire. Call him and tell him I must reach him. If he's been listening to the radio or TV, he'll know who I am."

"Oh, *that* Mr. Quist," the girl said. She had been listening.

"I'll give you a number for him to call," Quist said. "I'll be here for ten minutes, not a second longer. If he doesn't call, you can tell Mr. Wilshire that when I catch up with him I will take him apart, limb from limb! So move, young lady."

64

Quist asked Jason, the houseman, to find Officer Callahan, the motorcycle cop who was outside with the police contingent. Callahan appeared, a broad grin on his Irish face.

"Bracing yourself for the ride back, Mr. Quist?"

"Can we make it in fifty minutes? I want to be there when Captain Haller makes contact."

"More like thirty-five," Callahan said, ". . . if you can stand the pressure."

"I'm waiting for a call," Quist said. "I've given them until ten after nine—six more minutes."

"Piece of cake if we start by then," Callahan said.

At eight minutes past the phone rang. Jason answered, and then handed the phone to Quist. "Mr. Wilshire for you, sir," he said.

Quist took the phone. "Martin Wilshire?"

"I'm calling, Mr. Quist, not because I felt intimidated by your message, but because I'm curious." It was a suave, cultivated, slightly mocking voice. The Reapers, Quist thought, went for expensive talent.

"I have just two minutes, Wilshire," Quist said.

"Heading back to the Complex for the negotiations?" Wilshire asked.

"So you know what's cooking out there?"

"I've had my television set on for the last two hours. Quite a drama."

"I need to talk to you about the Reapers. Will you come out to the Complex, or do I come back to town after Captain Haller has talked with them?"

"In the minute and a half we have, I will tell you all I can, Mr. Quist—which, in effect, is nothing. The Reapers have been my clients. Anything I know about them is covered by lawyer-client confidentiality."

"You know a man named Smith?"

"That I think I can answer," Wilshire said. "There may

be a man named Smith, but if there is he doesn't use that name. In the Reapers' vocabulary Smith is the equivalent of general, Brown the equivalent of major, Jones the equivalent of captain. The man at the Complex who calls himself Smith could be any one of several hundred top-level members of the cult."

"Is there anyone who handles public relations for these people?"

Wilshire chuckled. "The equivalent of Quist?" he asked. "The Reapers are a very carefully organized group, my friend. Nobody handles the same job twice running. I gather what I've been hearing on television has been released by them, but I wouldn't have the faintest idea who is handling it."

Quist's voice was harsh. "Who is the Great White Father, the Ayatollah, the head bullshit artist?" he asked.

Wilshire was obviously amused. His laughter was soft. "Simeon Taylor, long dead, is the symbolic leader, as Jesus Christ is of the Christian church," he said.

"The living leader?" Quist insisted.

"My dear Mr. Quist, I'm not a member of the Reapers, I just handle their legal affairs. When I have to deal with somebody, his name is Smith. Just a general, you understand."

"I'll be getting back to you," Quist said.

"Any time," Wilshire said. "I'll leave word with my secretary to put you through whenever you call."

"Thanks—for nothing," Quist said.

"Good luck to your Miss Morton," Wilshire said.

Callahan's wailing siren was a cure for anxiety. The race out the expressway to the Complex required so much attention to driving that there was no time to think of anything but getting there in one piece. It was exactly a quarter to ten when Quist, flexing tensed hands, walked into Garvey's office where Haller and the others were

66

watching the hands of the electric clock move toward the moment of contact. He had left Connie Parmalee behind to go through Judge Padgett's voluminous files on the Paul Kramer trial.

"Anything from inside?" he asked.

Haller shook his head. Dan Garvey moved over to stand by his friend. "It's going to be okay for quite a while still, Julian," he said. "Lydia's probably taking it a lot better than we are."

"The judge, Mr. Quist?" Haller asked.

Quist described a courageous old man, perhaps more afraid of Lefty Orso than he was of the Reapers. "He even suggested giving himself up."

"Without Zorn that could mean we'd get half the hostages back," Kreevich said. He was standing at the desk, still involved with the blueprints the architect had left. "His records? I arranged for them to be delivered. Did they get there in time?"

"Yes, but they're not promising. Just legal points made during the long trial. My secretary's going through them. Could take a couple of days, for God's sake."

"We still haven't located or heard from Carl Zorn."

"I talked to Martin Wilshire on the phone," Quist said. "The sonofabitch found the whole situation rather amusing, I think. About all I got out of him is that Smith is just a title, like general."

Haller drew a deep breath. "Well, gentlemen, we're about there. I'll have the squawk box on here so that you can all hear the conversation with Smith, but I urge that none of you break in with questions or comments. For the moment I want it to be just between him and me. I don't want him to think he's putting on a show for all of you." He glanced at Quist. "Please don't ask about Miss Morton. What he would tell you wouldn't mean very much at best." He glanced at his watch. "A minute and a half," he said.

They all stood there, attention riveted on the electric clock—Quist, Kreevich, Dan Garvey, Captain Jansen of the state troopers, and Vic Lorch. The clock moved on, each motion of the second hand a little nervous jump.

At precisely ten o'clock Haller lifted the receiver and began dialing. The phone on the other end could only have rung once, before Smith's voice came through to them.

"Good morning, Captain," he said. "I'm eager to hear your sad story, whatever it may be."

Part Two

1 "How are the hostages doing, Smith?" Haller asked. It could have been asked on the street corner, about somebody's family. No real concern or emotion.

"Some better than others," the voice said—the voice named Smith. "There are those who want to get home to their mommies, and there are those who are grown up. Only the kitchen helper I mentioned earlier is hurt at all. Fortunately one of the hostages appears to be a reasonably competent doctor. All the comforts of home, Captain. So, how is your world?"

"Moving rather slowly," Haller said. "I'm sure you know that we could raise an astronomical amount of ransom money for you."

"Oh, I know, Captain. You'd be surprised at the offers I've had from people inside here. It's astonishing the value in cash that people put on their lives. Cash is not what I want, however, My price is still two men. You haven't mentioned them."

"What can I tell you?" Haller asked. He sounded casual, yet Quist could see that the knuckles on a closed fist were white. "We know where Judge Padgett is. So far we haven't located Carl Zorn, nor has he communicated with us. You know that you have some of Lefty Orso's people in there?"

"Of course I know. Oh my, do they talk big. We've had to tape one of their mouths shut with adhesive. His language was offending our lady guests."

"Orso has been here," Haller said. "He threatens to deliver the judge and Mr. Zorn to you, dead if necessary, if we don't solve the problem."

Smith's voice seemed to harden. "Tell Orso for me that I

71

don't want them dead. I want them to face our people, stand trial, hear the charges against them, try to defend themselves before we pass sentence on them. Anything less than that and we'll have failed in our mission, and all his people, and all your people, and all my people will die in one big holocaust."

"You do realize that every damned person in this country, from the president on down to the raggedest bagwoman in the city slums, knows there is no way on earth we can turn over two men to you to murder?"

"But you are willing to turn over three hundred and twenty-six people to us to murder? That really doesn't make much sense, does it, Captain? I know it may take a little while for you, and the president, and the governor, and the mayor, and all the bagwomen east of the Mississippi to assess the values in the situation. You all may decide that a soft-headed judge and a venal prosecutor are worth more than three hundred and twenty-six relatively innocent people. If you do, you'll have only yourselves to blame for what I guarantee will happen."

"I have to think you have a second choice for us in mind, knowing that we can't meet your number one demand," Haller said.

"The trouble with you, Captain," Smith said, "and the president, and all the rest of the authorities out there, is that you have no concept of justice, of morality, of biblical law. 'An eye for an eye, a tooth for a tooth.' 'As ye sow, so shall ye reap.' The System killed a man who in our eyes was a saint. The System must pay for that. The price is two people in exchange for three hundred and twenty-six. I know what your job is, Captain, representing the System. It is to talk and talk and talk, until I make you a better deal, or until your cops, your troopers, perhaps even the army, think they have devised a way to make a successful attack on this building. Let them try, and I promise you we'll blow this place and everyone in it sky high."

"Your people?" Haller asked.

"My people. There are fifty-two of them in here, so you see there are three hundred and seventy-eight of us in all. You attack and we are prepared to die along with the hostages. The price for failure, in our case, is death. I think that makes it as clear as I can make it, Captain. Now there isn't much point in our continuing this conversation. I'll give you and your high mucky-mucks in the System some time to arrive at a sensible decision. I know people in authority are unable to make snap decisions, because they care more about what other people think of them, what voters think of them, than what God thinks of them."

"How much more time?" Haller asked. "It will take quite a while for me to convey your message to people who can make the decision."

"I know, Captain. But there are limits to my patience. Keep in touch with me from time to time, let me know how things are progressing. I'll let you know how my patience is holding out. I think that's all for now. I hope I've persuaded you that you have no options. And I hope you'll persuade Lefty Orso that his people, three men and their broads, will be the first to go if he tries to get into the act."

The dial tone was like a dentist's drill when Smith disconnected at his end.

Haller leaned back in his chair. There were little beads of perspiration on his forehead and upper lip.

"So, we have some more time," he said, reaching for a handkerchief in his hip pocket.

"He's totally off his rocker," Dan Garvey said. He glanced at Quist who looked frozen to the spot where he stood.

"I got no less than I hoped for in the first conversation,"

73

Haller said. "He may be crazy, but he's also a realist. He knows I'm just a bargainer, without authority. He hoped to convince me of his position. He knows I have to carry it to someone else for an answer, and that the answer won't come in a hurry."

"Are you convinced?" Quist asked. His voice sounded far away.

"I have been dealing with the demands of crazies for a good twenty years," Haller said. "They almost always mean what they say the first time around. After the second, or the third, or the fourth talk they may be convinced that they have to take less than they asked for."

"Such as?" Quist asked.

"Money," Haller said. "A chance for him and his fifty-two friends to get away free, no punishment, no criminal charges, a plane to take them somewhere."

"Will you be authorized to do that?" Quist asked.

"To save three hundred and twenty-six lives? I think so," Haller said. "After the big shots stop trying to look like heroes."

"So what do we do? I mean *me*," Quist said.

"I told you earlier, Mr. Quist, I hope for some kind of successful Judas hunt—given time. You have Judge Padgett and his files. You've made a contact with Martin Wilshire. One or the other—or both of them—may lead us to the Reaper organization away from this point of action. We'll catch up with Zorn, who may be even more helpful. Somewhere, I'm convinced, inside the Reapers' cult, is someone who knows where their money comes from and who really is cleaning up—someone who isn't concerned with justice, and morality, and biblical law. Someone who is using dedicated young people, infected by some kind of phony ministry, someone dishing out some kind of cynical double-talk. That person may be willing to give us what we need to turn those kids in the Stirrup Cup against their

74

general—Smith—if we'll pay enough. Money isn't our problem. We can raise almost anything that's asked if it will free those people in there."

"The person who bothers me," Lieutenant Kreevich said, "is the guy sitting in there with his hand on the detonator that will blow the place up. He has to be convinced, because it will only take one second for him to push down on that plunger."

Quist started for the door.

"I'll go with you," Kreevich said. "If the answer is in the city, that's my beat." He stopped by Haller. "Keep pitching, Captain. So far you're showing us some pretty good stuff."

"Your people in the city may help us locate Zorn," Haller said. "If anyone can get us to the center of the Reapers, he's it. He spent almost a year digging before the Kramer trial. He did have cops guarding him for a while. They may know his habits, his secret places. His office just says he's 'out of town.'"

Lydia was just inside the dark clapboarding on that building, almost close enough for him to talk to if he raised his voice. The troopers, the police, the security men who encircled the place were, Quist thought, actually protecting the villains. Containment, Haller had called it.

"I know what you're thinking," Kreevich said, standing by his friend. "But fifty-two people with sophisticated weapons could make a shepherd's pie out of you if you decided to try to be a hero."

Quist squared back his shoulders and looked up at the sky, away from the shuttered windows of the Stirrup Cup. It was a perfect summer day, only a few fleecy clouds in the blue, the sun comfortingly warm. All around the grounds of the Complex there were flowers and shrubs in bloom. Some distance away a man rode a lawn mower, as though it was any day. Quist heard a rumbling sound and after a moment recognized it as the thunder of galloping horses on the racetrack just a few yards away. The thoroughbreds had to have their morning workouts, hostage crisis or no hostage crisis. Except for the army of the press, gathered around their improvised coffee and food stand, it could have been just any day. Vic Lorch's men and the cops had managed to keep the area clear of curious crowds who had no legitimate business there. There were many cars in the parking lot, which suggested that families of hostages, their lawyers, politicians, city and county officials, had been herded into the main arena building to shout their demands and wait for news.

"It makes just as little sense to them as it does to you," Kreevich said. "Why *my* husband, *my* brother, *my* daughter? Why Lydia? They just happened to be there when the world spun off its axis."

"Let's get out of here," Quist said. He took a last look at the captured building and headed for the parking lot and his car.

They drove toward the city, this time without Officer Callahan as an outrider.

"'Use my head' you told me a while back," Quist said when they were on the expressway. "I don't know how to use it, Mark. I never felt so goddamned alone and without direction in all my life! We're headed for what—eight million people? We're supposed to find one man—a Judas—who will sell out his friends for a price. Where the hell do we look? Is he black, white, already rich, poor? One man in eight million!"

"In my business I'm faced with that kind of dilemma almost every day," Kreevich said. "A human being is murdered and we look for the killer, one man or woman in a city of eight million."

"But you have a starting point," Quist said. "You have a

victim, and he had a family, business associates, a woman or women. You have an area in which to start looking."

"Unless he was just mugged for his wallet," Kreevich said. "In this case we know the motive: revenge. We know that it springs from a relatively small community of people, a fraternity, a congregation. Somewhere there is information about them, where they live, where they gather. We may be provided with that when we hit the city. There may be details in the judge's files. When we locate Zorn he should be loaded with the kind of detail we need. There must be a way to persuade Martin Wilshire to give. And there's one happy thing about it so far, Julian. Nobody is dead—yet."

"Except a 'saint' who hanged himself in a jail cell," Quist said.

"Just know that we're not trying for the impossible, chum," Kreevich said.

"If that bastard in the Cup gives us enough time," Quist said.

"Don't sell Haller short," Kreevich said. "He's talked a hell of a lot of people into time in his career. He's good at it."

Quist pounded on the steering wheel with his left hand. "Using innocent people like poker chips in a crooked card game!" he said.

"It's getting to be the number-one crime in the world today," Kreevich said. "Would you like to guess how many hostage situations are going on around the globe right at this minute? You haven't read the newspaper this morning, but if you had you'd probably find that someone is holding a missionary in Central America, that a planeload of innocent people are being held hostage in the Middle East, that an Italian politician is in the hands of terrorists in Rome, that a whole settlement is under the gun in the Third World, and beyond that every kidnapping, and they happen every day, is a hostage case. It's become a way of life—a way to get rich, the way to win a revolution, to fight a war, to overthrow a dictator, to get your friends out of jail. But take comfort from the fact that it happens so frequently that men like Captain Haller are trained to deal with it. A hostage negotiating team is a fact of life. Never was such a unit a few years back. Now they're involved every day."

"How often do they succeed?"

"Their record's pretty good. When you're dealing with a lone lunatic it's touch and go. When you're dealing with a political group, an organized group like the Reapers, there's usually a better chance. You hope they're asking for more than they really expect to get, and that you can make a deal for less."

"You think that's the situation out there at the Cup?"

Kreevich gave his friend a quick, sideways glance. "Fifty-two hopped-up fanatics are hard to assess," he said. "If we can find a Judas, we may come up with a lesser deal that they'll buy."

"So you're not optimistic?"

"I'm not going to sit on my behind and wait to see what happens," Kreevich said. "Nor are you, I hope."

The street outside Judge Padgett's brownstone on Murray Hill looked like a parking lot for police cars. Both the Park Avenue and Lexington Avenue ends of the block were shut off, and black-and-whites were parked all the way through the block on both sides of the street. Blue uniforms made it look like a cop convention.

Kreevich's authority got them straight through to the front door of the judge's house where Sergeant Kaminski, alerted by a walkie-talkie, was waiting to greet them.

"Looks like the judge was safe three times over," Kreevich said.

"Lot of ground to cover," Kaminski said. "Occupants of all the houses in this block and the block behind, rooftops for snipers. We've got bomb experts going over adjoining houses. If the Reapers are using explosives out there at the Complex, they could try them here, too."

"I think they have a special drama planned for the judge and Zorn," Kreevich said.

"There's Lefty Orso, too," Kaminski said. "He's got an army he can call on, you know. He'll go pretty far to get his people out at the Cup released. Underworld rule. You don't let your own people hang out to dry somewhere."

Jason Brinker, the judge's houseman, let Quist and Kreevich into the house. Kaminski had given him the all-clear through the intercom system in the foyer panel.

"The judge is in his study," Jason said. "There's something on the TV about the situation at the Complex."

The judge was leaning forward in an armchair, watching the television set. He gestured to Quist and Kreevich, indicating they should listen.

A familiar TV reporter was interviewing Joel Broadhurst, the steel company executive whose wife was one of the hostages in the Cup.

"And so, Mr. Broadhurst, since the Reapers' demands can't be met, what is the next move?" the reporter asked.

There was a twitch at the corners of Broadhurst's jowly mouth. "Money. We can raise enough money to support them for the next ten years."

"You're talking in the thousands?"

"More."

"Hundreds of thousands?"

"More," Broadhurst said, as casually as if he was talking about the jelly beans in President Reagan's desk jar.

"They've said they're not interested in money," the reporter said.

"You know anyone who, in the final analysis, isn't?"

"But if they refuse? If they insist on having Judge Padgett and Carl Zorn turned over to them?"

"Which can't, of course, be done."

"But if they refuse anything else?"

Again the loose mouth twitched at its corners. "There are several thousand members of the Reapers scattered all over the country. The police and the FBI should take as many of them as they can get to, *in the next hour*, and hold them as—as counterhostages. That's their motto, isn't it? An eye for an eye?"

"Damn fool," Judge Padgett muttered. "A Presbyterian minister screws a choir singer and all Presbyterians should be arrested and charged with rape!"

The interviewer seemed to realize he was on touchy ground. He shifted gears. "You'd be willing to pay ransom for your wife's release?" he asked.

Broadhurst looked straight into the camera. "On the chance that they're listening I make an offer here and now," he said. "I will pay five hundred thousand dollars for my wife's safe release."

"And the other three hundred and twenty-five hostages?"

"They have their own people to make their own offers," Broadhurst said.

"Well, thank you, Mr. Broadhurst. We wish you a safe outcome of this tense and tragic situation. It is almost certain that your offer has been heard and, we hope, given serious consideration. And now we take you back to the Island Complex and our crew there."

Judge Padgett leaned forward and switched off the set. Quist introduced Kreevich.

"The lieutenant and I are old acquaintances," the judge said. "He's appeared in my court more than once."

"I'm flattered that you remember, Your Honor," Kreevich said.

80

The judge smiled at him. "I always remember competence," he said. "I take it you two have just come from the Complex?"

"Nothing moving so far," Kreevich said. "Haller had his first talk with Smith at ten o'clock. No change in the demands."

"What is being done?" The judge was quite cool for a man who knew his own life was on the line.

"Obviously, Your Honor, you and Mr. Zorn will be protected. A lot of hysterical suggestions are being made by the general public, by relatives and friends of the hostages. One of them you can be quite sure won't be implemented. You and Mr. Zorn will not be exchanged for anyone."

"If money is the answer, I'd do what I could to help raise a ransom," the judge said.

"Money isn't the answer—yet," Kreevich said.

"You've contacted Zorn?"

"We hadn't when we left the Complex about forty minutes ago. If I could use your phone to call my office—"

The judge gestured toward the phone on the desk across the room. He looked at Quist. "Anything from inside the Cup?" he asked. "Anything about your lady, Mr. Quist?"

Quist shook his head.

The judge looked down at his heavily veined hands. "I've had many murderers in my courtroom," he said. "Men who murdered their wives, wives who murdered their husbands. I've often felt sympathy for those killers because I thought I understood the pressures and tensions that had produced the passion to kill. But when a totally innocent, unconnected person is threatened, used as a bargaining chip, then I feel no impulse toward mercy, no compassion. Did you follow the Kramer case, Mr. Quist?"

"No," Quist said. "Oh, the headlines. Kramer killed a government lawyer, am I right?"

The judge nodded. "No question about it. Kramer killed him, murdered him. The dead man had been trying to build a case against Kramer—grand larceny, the misappropriation of Reaper funds for his own personal use. The FBI has been trying to find something on the Reapers, or people high up in the Reaper command. They thought they had it. And then Kramer walked into this lawyer's office and shot him dead at his desk. He never denied it. Hell, there were witnesses." The judge's eyebrows drew together in a frown. "But something about it had a sour taste for me. Kramer was an educated man. Maybe he was a clever thief. But I could never understand why he would walk into a man's office, gun him down in the presence of screaming secretaries and office boys, and then wait, calmly, for the police to come and take him. There had to be a motive beyond the simple business of a larceny case against him that hadn't yet gotten as far as a grand jury. My instinct kept telling me that Kramer murdered that lawyer for some personal reason. But it never came out. I had Martin Wilshire in my chambers during the trial. I suggested to him that his client was holding back something. He almost admitted that was true, but not quite. A bitter little smile that suggested I was on to something. Nothing ever came of it. Kramer took the stand, said he'd killed the dead man because he was trying to discredit him in the cult to which he was dedicated—the Reapers. That was it. Open and shut. The jury convicted him, couldn't have done otherwise. The sentence for murder is mandatory—fifteen to life. I had no options. I didn't impose a heavy sentence on Kramer; it was the only sentence the law allows. Zorn didn't win his case by some kind of legal trickery. He had a murder, with half a dozen eyewitnesses—period." The judge shook his head. "Why do the Reapers want to punish us? We were officers of the court, doing what was a very simple, straightforward, uncomplicated job."

Kreevich came back from the telephone. There was nothing yet on Zorn.

"I always had a theory about the Kramer case," he said. He lit one of his endless chain of cigarettes. "I figured that lawyer—O'Brien was his name, wasn't it—was going to wrap up Kramer like a Christmas package on the larceny charge. In his world, the self-righteous world of the Reapers, anything was better than being convicted of stealing—stealing the Reapers' own funds. He chose to take another rap, murder. The facts about thievery were buried. All anybody cared about was getting Kramer for murder. The FBI probably had him framed on the larceny charge. That's the way they've so often done business since the days when the late J. Edgar Hoover used to find ways to get people he didn't like. They weren't able to smear Kramer and the Reaper command as they'd hoped, but the murder got Kramer out of their hair."

"Interesting, but do you have a shred of evidence?" the judge asked.

"No, Your Honor. But I felt uneasy about the case, as you did, and I invented an explanation so I could stop thinking about it."

"You can forget it, but nobody is out to get you because of it," the judge said.

"I promise you, Your Honor, their chances of getting to you are about ninety-nine to one against it."

"I hope you're right, Lieutenant," the judge said. He moved stiff shoulders in an effort to relax. "Your Miss Parmalee is in the living room, working at the files, Quist. Nice girl. Long and rather futile paper chase, I'm afraid. If there was anything there that would reveal something unexpected about the Kramer case, I'd have spotted it long ago. All she's really got are endless rulings on exceptions taken by the defense."

"Martin Wilshire?"

"Yes. He knew he was fighting a losing cause. He took

exception to almost every ruling I made, about the admissibility of evidence, about the propriety of a witness testifying, about a certain fact, about simple legal procedure. His hope was that my foot would slip somewhere, just out of impatience, give him grounds for an appeal. I'm happy to say the appeals court didn't uphold him on a single point."

"Job well done," Kreevich said.

"It wasn't that tricky," the judge said.

Connie Parmalee looked relieved to see Quist. "You should have a legal secretary going through this, Julian," she said. "I don't understand the whys and wherefores of half of it—legal mumbo jumbo. If you want to really know about Kramer, you probably need a transcript of the trial, everything day by day. This just shows you that the judge is a professional who knows his stuff."

"Zorn's our man," Quist said, "if he'd just pop out of his rabbit hole."

You could walk into any bar or restaurant anywhere in the city and the television set would keep you posted on the Stirrup Cup hostages. The radio in any taxicab would keep you up to date, with editorial comment from the driver. Opinions ranged from turning the judge and Zorn over and getting the hostages out, to storming the place, with the army if necessary, and to hell with who got killed as long as the Reapers were wiped out.

Quist had heard of a torture employed by South American terrorists: a rat in a tin can tied to a victims stomach, with no escape for the rat except to eat his way into the man's gut. Quist thought he knew what agony that must be like. He felt it almost every breath he took, between every sentence he spoke or that was spoken to him. Lydia! What was happening to her? What was happening to all the hostages? Were the fifty-two creeps

84

who were holding them mistreating them for kicks? What was he doing here, walking along Park Avenue in perfect safety, to Martin Wilshire's office? Why wasn't he back at the Cup, ready to charge in at the drop of a hat? What hat—whose hat?

He'd called before he had left the judge's and gotten Dan Garvey, his friend and partner, on the phone. Nothing stirring. There'd been no communication between Haller and Smith since Quist and Kreevich had set out for the city.

"You know what they say about 'no news,' pal," Garvey said.

"Here it's like swimming under water," Quist said. "Nothing moves, or is clear. I'm on my way to see Wilshire, Paul Kramer's lawyer. He could lead us somewhere if he will."

"Luck. And Julian, know that if there's any action out here—and Haller doesn't expect it—I'll be standing in for you in spades."

"If anything happens to Lydia—"

"I know, Julian."

Martin Wilshire's office was elegant, expensive. A receptionist told Quist he was expected and took him directly into Wilshire's private space. It was a moderately large, sunny room with windows looking out over Park Avenue. Much of the wall space was occupied by a calf-bound law library. Wilshire, sitting behind a large, very neat, flat-topped desk, was a "man of distinction," hair graying at his temples, tanned and healthy-looking, very bright blue eyes, a faintly sardonic smile. He was wearing an expensively tailored worsted summer suit, pale gray. He had an actor's mellow voice. A trial lawyer *is* an actor, Quist thought. He stood up and held out a hand to Quist. His handshake was firm, but not too firm.

"A grueling day for you, Mr. Quist," he said. He

85

gestured toward an expensive color TV set in a far corner. "I've been watching from time to time. Do sit down."

Quist felt anger growing in him. This man was the legal representative of the Reapers, the people who were holding Lydia.

"I had hoped that being willing to see you would make me seem a little less of a villain to you, Mr. Quist," the lawyer said.

"If you will help," Quist said.

"I'm limited in some respects by the lawyer-client code," Wilshire said. "Beyond that, anything. Know that I feel that what is going on out there at the Cup is an outrage."

"Yet when the time comes you'll defend those bastards in court?"

"Every man, no matter how evil or guilty, is entitled to a proper defense in the courts," Wilshire said.

Quist glanced around the office. "Particularly if he can afford the fee," he said.

Wilshire leaned back in his chair, a little mocking smile moving his lips. "Wouldn't it be more to your advantage, Mr. Quist, not to waste time with minor-league insults? No matter what you may feel about me, I assure you I haven't acted unethically in any fashion."

Quist drew a deep breath. That "rat" was gnawing at his stomach. Judge Padgett had made the same point for Wilshire earlier that day.

"We have only one chance that any of us can see, Wilshire," Quist said. "Somewhere in the Reapers' organization is someone who can provide us with a weapon to use in negotiating, something that might persuade them to settle for less. Money can be raised, possibly a plane to take them somewhere with freedom from prosecution."

"If they were to ask for my advice, I would suggest to them that they accept one of those lesser offers," Wilshire said. "Obviously nobody is going to turn Padgett or Zorn over to them." He gestured again toward the TV. "I heard Joel Broadhurst offering a half million dollars for his wife. A million or two for the lot, perhaps?"

"Are you bargaining for them, Wilshire?"

"Good God, no," the lawyer said. "Let me assure you that I haven't heard anything from anyone in that organization since this foolhardy business began. I would not be a party to it in any way."

"Smith again?"

"Just a title, as I told you on the phone. I might know him if I saw him. Can you describe him?"

"No. The only person we've talked to who was inside was blindfolded when he had contact with Smith."

"The man with emphysema?"

"Yes. A lawyer named Fahnestock."

Wilshire nodded. "Estate, not criminal. I know his reputation but not the man. So I can't help you with Smith."

"Give me a name," Quist said. "Someone at the top, someone who is genuinely religious and not a blackmailing fanatic. Someone who is remotely decent, who might see the mass murder of innocent people as something more than 'an eye for an eye.'"

Wilshire sat silent for a moment, frowning. "I have a problem you're going to find hard to believe," he said finally. "I don't have names. I handled the Kramer murder case. Paul Kramer is the only name I had that meant anything. I was hired by a Smith. My fees were delivered to me by a man named Brown—in cash. My client wasn't too cooperative; he seemed to want to be convicted. I tried to get help through Brown when he delivered money. Smith got back to me. He couldn't help."

"The only person you had direct contact with was Brown, who paid the bills? You could identify him, of course?"

"If I saw him again."

"Kramer never mentioned friends in the organization?"

"Secret as God," Wilshire said. "I tried to get character witnesses for him. He wouldn't name anyone."

"Surely the FBI, who set him up, must have names."

"Most of the names they have are their own. It was a scam. A setup. O'Brien, the lawyer Kramer shot, was part of the 'fix.' Kramer was offered money and freedom from prosecution on certain minor offenses if he would do what you are asking me to do—name the people at the top. Evidently Kramer was at least willing to listen. The FBI told me they had tapes of conversations that would prove that."

"You heard those tapes?"

"No. The charge was murder, with eyewitnesses. They didn't need anything but those witnesses to get a conviction. I tried to get the story of the scam introduced into the proceedings, but Judge Padgett ruled against it. I asked for time to find character witnesses for my client. The judge ruled against it. It didn't matter what Kramer's character had been. The simple fact was that Kramer had walked into O'Brien's office and shot him in full view of an office full of clerks and secretaries."

"The judge made it tough for you?"

"He's a damn good judge, Quist. I took a barrel full of exceptions to his rulings, but I didn't think appeals would back me up, and they didn't. Padgett knows his law. Zorn played it the best way possible as prosecutor. He never brought up the scam, never touched on motive. He had witnesses, he had a weapon that Kramer was licensed to carry. If you read the newspapers at the time, you'd have thought this was a trial about the Reapers. That is because the Smiths, the Joneses, and the Browns barraged the press with charges of persecution of a respected religious group. I hesitated getting it before the jury—that he was a Reaper. It might do him more harm than good, I thought."

The lawyer's smile was bitter. "Somehow the average man in the street isn't sympathetic to men who do God's work with a machine gun or a butcher knife."

"Kramer had a family—wife, children?"

He would never admit to a wife or a family. More important than that to me, Mr. Quist, is that he would never admit to me—even in confidence—that he killed O'Brien because he was part of a scam, a frameup. 'He was an evil man, and I was chosen as God's instrument to terminate him.' He said that to me over and over. He said it to Judge Padgett before he was sentenced. 'Do you have anything to say before I pass sentence?' 'He was an evil man. God chose me to deliver him for the Last Judgment.' You're wondering why I didn't plead insanity. Kramer wouldn't let me. 'I am saner than you are, Mr. Wilshire. You try to plead insanity and I will ask court to have you removed as my attorney.'"

"So he chose to get the works from the start, and hanged himself after he got what he wanted," Quist said. "Not a single friend?"

"Thousands of friends who call themselves Smith, Jones, and Brown," Wilshire said. "Fifty-two friends, one of them named Smith, holding those hostages out there in the Cup. Those people are crazy enough to do just what they threaten, Mr. Quist. God will tell them to murder those hostages if you don't produce Padgett and Zorn for them."

"And you won't help."

"I don't know how to help," Wilshire said, and Quist had to admit there was a ring of truth in the words.

"Advice, then," Quist said.

"What on earth can I advise you to do?" Wilshire said. He looked suddenly tired. "The so-called civilized community in which we live won't let you turn over two men to save over three hundred innocent men and women. Haller isn't going to be able to negotiate their freedom. He's over his head with those zealots. There's only one thing left. Plan quickly and carefully, storm the building, and save as many of them as you can. Hope that your Miss Morton is one of the lucky ones."

Quist's mouth had gone dry. "There's a man in there sitting with his hand on a plunger, ready to blow them all up—hostages and Reapers. You think the Reapers are ready to commit suicide?"

"I think they're just fanatical enough to do that." Wilshire said. "Find a way to eliminate that man at the detonator and you have a chance to save some of the hostages. Fail in that and God help you."

2 Quist had gone to Wilshire's office, convinced that he was tackling the enemy. He had come away with the certainty that the lawyer had played it pretty straight with him. Wilshire's cold assessment of the situation at the Cup reinforced his own feelings, which he had tried to keep from surfacing. Haller might gain them time, but in the end they were going to have to face an unthinkable violence. They were in the hands of madmen whose madness was frighteningly predictable.

Lydia!

Quist's office was only a couple of blocks from Wilshire's in a finger of glass pointing to the sky above Park Avenue. When he arrived and stepped off the elevator into his reception room he was faced with total disorder. The room was crowded with friends and clients, there to offer help, sympathy, and to satisfy curiosity. Miss Gloria Chard, the glamorous receptionist who usually kept things under complete control, was close to hysteria herself.

"Oh my God, Mr. Quist, is there any news?"

"None."

He almost had to fight his way through the crowd of friends, explaining that he had to call the Complex to get the latest report. In his own office, with its modern paintings and furnishings, he felt suddenly alone beyond endurance. No Lydia, no Connie Parmalee, who was still at Judge Padgett's. One of the girls from the secretarial pool followed him in.

"I don't know what to say, Mr. Quist."

"Get me the Complex on the phone, Leslie. Dan if he's available."

"There have been literally hundreds of calls for you, Mr. Quist," the girl said. "I've been trying to keep a list, but they come every minute. One in particular, though. Ossie Lord."

Ossie Lord was a black musician, a clarinetist who had a jazz group Quist had helped promote. They were called the "O Lords."

"Someday we'll catch up with all of them," Quist said. "What's particular about Ossie? Just another sympathetic friend."

The girl was at the telephone, having instructed the switchboard to call the Complex. She handed the instrument to Quist. "They're ringing," she said.

Garvey came on the other end. Nothing new, no change. Quist asked for Haller, but the captain was out of the office for the moment.

"Army people looking over the situation," Garvey said. "Just in case, you understand."

"I think I'm beginning to understand too well," Quist said. "That may be the only way, Dan."

"Keep your shirt on," Garvey said. "They have to know there's no way we can turn over the judge and Zorn. Haller warns all of us not to get trigger happy. He's certain that sooner or later the Reapers will come down a peg in their demands and then *that* will have to be negotiated. Everything takes time—and the patience to wait it out."

"Ask Haller to call me at the office when he's free. I've been to see Wilshire. Finding a Judas may not be in the rolling-off-a-log department."

"Will do," Garvey said. "And take it easy, pal. The real heat isn't on yet. You're going to need all the guts you've got when the time comes."

"If I have any guts when the rat gets through with me," Quist said.

"What rat?"

Quist's laugh was grim. "I'll tell you sometime. It's a joke about man's inhumanity to man. Thanks for just being out there, Dan."

"I can't really say 'it's my pleasure,'" Garvey said.

Quist put down the phone. Leslie, the stand-in secretary, was still standing across the desk from him.

"About Ossie Lord," she said.

"You like his music, you'd like to do him a favor," Quist said.

"If Connie were here you'd believe her in a second," the girl said. "I just have a feeling about Ossie, Mr. Quist."

"I've got a lot on my mind, babe," Quist said. "Words of one syllable, please."

"Ossie wants you to call. He's sitting by his phone. He says he has something that might help at the Cup. I didn't think it was a trick to get to talk to you."

"You got a number? Call him," Quist said. "Sorry if I was short with you, Leslie. The pressures are a little heavy."

The girl was already dialing a number she had written on her steno pad. The answer was instant and she handed Quist the phone after identifying the call.

"Ossie?" Quist said.

"Oh, man, you got yourself trouble," Ossie Lord said. There were overtones of the late Louis Armstrong in Ossie's scratchy voice. "Maybe I can help."

"How, Ossie?"

"Maybe I flatter myself when I think you must be thinkin' the way I am," Ossie said. "If I was you, man, I'd be tryin' to get at some Reapers that ain't inside the Cup."

"With some name other than Smith, Jones, or Brown," Quist said.

"I got one for you, man. Two, as a matter of fact—though you won't be able to talk to Number Two, I guess. Would you believe he's locked up out there in the Cup with the rest of the hostages? Pete Damon, a piano player. Black like me."

"He's a Reaper?"

"Is—at least was. Played with the O Lords for a while. He'd talk a little too much when he was on coke."

"Cocaine?"

"Oh, man! Ate it, sniffed it, took a bath in it—whatever. Someone in the Reapers was his dealer. That's how they keep most of their crazy people in line."

Quist found himself instantly thinking about Sally Craven, the red-haired girl singer for whom Pete Damon had been playing at the Cup. Could she have been the person on the outside passing information about who was where and doing what to someone on the inside in that first hour, before the phones were shut off?

"It's not Pete I called you about," Ossie Lord said. "If I tell you I may lose a friend, someone I admire and respect. But those crazy bastards have all those people, and your woman."

"Who is it, Ossie?"

"Here goes nothin'," Ossie said. "It's Dyanne Jordan."

It took Quist seconds to put a face to the name. Dyanne Jordan—beautiful black girl singer of blues and jazz classics, a young Lena Horne, very near the top of the entertainment ladder. "She's a Reaper?" Quist asked.

"Oh, man, not Dyanne. You sitting down, Julian? Dyanne is—was—Paul Kramer's lady."

"He wasn't black," Quist said.

"You're my friend and you're not black," Ossie said.

"You know her well?"

"Sure. She toured with the O Lords for more than a year, all over this country, Europe, Australia. We been close for a long time. She's the best at what she does, you know."

"Those people out at the Cup are trying to get even for Paul Kramer. Why would Dyanne want to help me?"

"Because she's a decent human being. Because I'd promise her you wouldn't involve her with the cops, or with the Reapers. She might tell you things you could use, but you couldn't drag her into it. You promise me, Julian, and I'll take you to her."

"You know I'll promise you," Quist said. "I have to. Lydia—"

"I know, man. I know. I'll meet you in the lobby of the Beaumont Hotel as soon as you can make it."

Quist glanced at his watch. "Fifteen minutes," he said.

The Beaumont, New York's top luxury hotel, was an old stamping ground of Quist's. Doormen, bell captains, bartenders, maitre d's, normally greeted him as an old friend and a valued customer. Today he was a celebrity because of what was going on out at the Cup. He hadn't anticipated being surrounded by the curious and the sympathetic as he walked into the lobby. Neither had Ossie Lord.

The musician was standing at the far end of the lobby near the bank of elevators. He made an eloquent little gesture to Quist suggesting that they not recognize each other, stepped into an elevator, and disappeared.

Quist, swarmed over by hundreds of questions, felt someone pressing something into his hand. He turned and recognized the hotel's day bell captain. In Quist's hand was a crumpled piece of paper. On it was written a number— 1411. A room number, of course. The bell captain smiled at him and moved away.

It took Quist a good ten minutes to work his way to an elevator and get himself whisked up to the fourteenth floor. Ossie was waiting for him when he stepped out.

"I never dreamed—" he said.

"The best way to get famous is to have trouble," Quist said. "Dyanne Jordan is in 1411?"

"The bell captain is an old friend," Ossie said.

"The lady knows you're bringing me?"

Ossie grinned. "She doesn't even know I'm bringing me," he said. "She's glued to her TV set in there, like half the city. I didn't call her. She'd have said no."

Ossie rang the bell at 1411, and after a moment or two the door was opened and they were confronted by Dyanne Jordan. A beautiful woman, Quist thought, skin the color of dark honey, black hair, bright black eyes, a figure that would have been a high-fashion model's dream.

"Ossie," she said, and then her pleasure evaporated as she looked at Quist. She was like a movie fan who sees a familiar face and can't remember what film she'd seen it in. Then her expressive eyes narrowed. "You're Julian Quist! I've just been watching—" She turned to Ossie. "You had no right—"

"A good friend—in trouble," Ossie said.

Dyanne started to close the door, but Ossie managed to wedge a shoulder in the opening. "I promise, Dyanne, no cops, no Reapers. Just help. He needs it bad."

"I, too, promise, Miss Jordan," Quist said.

"You don't have any idea what you're asking," Dyanne said.

"I'm asking for help to save the most precious person in the world to me," Quist said.

It was as if she needed to think of a dozen answers, and then she stepped back from the door and Ossie walked in with Quist behind him.

It was a typical Beaumont suite, elegantly furnished in a period—this one early American. There was a beautiful painting hung on the center wall, a Benton, Quist guessed. The only thing out of period was the television set flickering in the corner. At the moment it was showing some kind of game show, and Dyanne had turned down the sound, waiting for the network to cut away and go back to the Stirrup Cup.

The two men waited for Dyanne to suggest sitting. For a moment or two she might not have known they were there. She walked over to the windows that overlooked Central Park, bathed in the afternoon sun. Finally she turned and faced them. *Beauty* wasn't a word that Quist used casually in connection with women. It meant more to him than the bone structure of a face, a wide generous mouth, the texture of skin, a graceful and eye-catching figure. It was some kind of illumination from the inside, some kind of spirit and courage shining through, something that suggested a mystery you'd give anything to solve. Lydia had it. That dark-skinned woman, facing him, had it. He remembered being enchanted by her singing on stage, in a night club, in a couple of television specials. She could make a blues song sound like a hymn, or an operatic aria, or a cribside lullaby—whatever she chose. He'd thought that was acting, technique, something she'd trained and studied to achieve. But she wasn't acting now, and that inner mystery, that genuine beauty, was shining brightly.

"I should ask you to go," she said.

"I hope that word *should* means that you won't, Miss Jordan," Quist said.

"Do you have any prejudice against a white man and a black woman being in love, Mr. Quist?" she asked.

"None."

"Just like that?"

"You mean that I can answer without hesitation? The only prejudice I have is against the wrong people being together for the wrong reasons. I never knew Paul Kramer. I know little or nothing about him. I have seen your work and admire you enormously. His color or your color would have nothing whatever to do with any judgments I might make about your relationship."

"Julian isn't whitey, Dyanne," Ossie said. "I wouldn't have brought him here if he was. And the Reapers are all the colors of the rainbow. None of this has got anything to do with white or black."

She took a deep breath. "Please sit down, both of you."

The first skirmish had been won. Quist and Ossie sat down on opposite ends of the upholstered couch, Dyanne remained standing behind a maple armchair, her hands gripping the top slat of its back.

"There really isn't anything you can say to a person who is watching a loved one hang from the edge of a cliff by her fingernails," Dyanne said.

"Meaning Lydia?"

"Meaning your Miss Morton, and the three hundred and twenty-five other people who belong to someone."

"Perhaps you can understand that it's hard for me to think of anyone out there but my woman," Quist said. "But if I can find a way to help her, it will help the others, too."

"What is it you think I can do for you, Mr. Quist?"

"This situation, at least on the surface, is all about Paul Kramer," Quist said. "He was one of them—one of the Reapers. In retaliation for his trial, conviction, sentencing, and eventual suicide, the Reapers are asking for two men whom they plan to execute. Obviously the community won't turn over those two men. We have to find some way to bargain with them for less. But perhaps you think Judge Padgett and Carl Zorn deserve the kind of punishment planned for them."

"Good God no!" Dyanne said.

"They did in Paul Kramer, drove him to suicide."

"Paul did himself in," the woman said. "He killed Francis O'Brien; the punishment handed down by the court was no more nor less than the System demands. Paul couldn't face the prospect of years in jail—perhaps forever."

"You feel no resentment against the judge and the prosecutor?"

"No more than I feel against a traffic light that turns red when I've driving down a highway. It's part of the System."

"You sympathize with the Reapers?"

"Sow death, reap death?"

"Yes."

"No! Not now, not ever."

"Paul Kramer was at the top. You must know others who are at the top."

Dyanne moved away from the chair to which she'd been clinging and turned to the window once more. Quist fought to control a terrible impatience. Time was running out, like sand through an hourglass. Smith, the Reapers' general at the Cup, might decide to speed things up by presenting Captain Haller with a dead hostage in the trash. He'd suggested that possibility.

"Paul had a sister," Dyanne said, her back still turned to her visitors. "She was born autistic."

"What's autistic?" Ossie asked.

Dyanne turned. "The dictionary calls autism a 'preoccupation with fantasy as opposed to any interest in reality,'" she said. "Some people would just say 'retarded.' Mildred Kramer had no notions of reality. She could barely

98

communicate such needs as hunger, or thirst, or the need to go to the bathroom. Today she can't communicate at all. She is in what you might call an 'awake coma.' There are fantasies locked away inside her, but God knows what they are. They could be terrible nightmares."

"The Reapers, Dyanne. I need to know about the Reapers!" Quist said.

"Ten years ago," Dyanne said, as if she hadn't heard Quist speak, "Paul's parents had both died, leaving him as Mildred's only living relative. She was twelve years old at the time, a beautiful blank-faced child. Paul was a successful computer operator, setting up systems for big companies all over the country. He had the money for the very best medical care for Milly, but the doctors didn't produce any results. About that time someone told Paul about Simeon Taylor. He was the founder of the Reapers. He was, I truly believe, a deeply religious man. Off base, but believing his particular rules of morality and justice. Paul told me then he thought the man was a phony—Paul and I had just found each other ten years ago. Simeon was a phony, Paul thought, but there was talk everywhere that he could perform miracles of healing. What could be lost by seeing if Simeon could do anything for Milly?"

"And could he?" Quist asked, trying to move it on.

"You would have had to see it to believe it," Dyanne said. "Milly was going on thirteen and she began reacting to things like a four year old—but a normal, bright, intelligent four year old. And then Simeon was killed. Milly didn't go backward, but she didn't go any further forward either. It appeared she was going to stay four years old forever. But that was far better than a blank."

"Who took over for Simeon Taylor?"

"In the Reapers? Like any organization that's been centered around one man there was a struggle, a lot of people trying to swim to the top. Paul, I guess, was one of them."

"He had joined them?"

"When Milly began to show signs of being a human being I guess Paul would have done anything for them. What he was able to do well for them, especially with his own contacts, was raise money. And he was glad to do it. For what Simeon Taylor had done for Milly he felt he owed them, and while the old man was still alive Paul had no complaints. He didn't believe in their 'Sow death, reap death' credo, but they did good things for people— underprivileged people, blacks, Puerto Ricans, other minorities. No one pointed a finger at him and laughed at him, a white man living with a black woman. Because we were living together by then. Paul hated the drugs that were a big part of the scene, but drugs are everywhere today, in all strata of society. From Hollywood to Harlem we're living in a drug-infected world.

"Anyway, it was Paul who swam to the top after the old man was killed. I don't know, Mr. Quist, but I guess I'd have to say he bought some of the violence the old man had taught. You had to lash back against a corrupt system. They were always talking about the System."

"'They'?" Quist asked.

Her laugh was bitter. "It's an organization of Smiths, Joneses, and Browns. Didn't you know that, Mr. Quist? Paul was the head Smith. I—I didn't believe in any of it, and yet Paul and I stayed so very close. I had my own career—tours, concerts, records, engagements in Vegas and New York and even in Europe. I toured with Ossie and his O Lords, you know. So what Paul and I had wasn't like a marriage or even a live-together. I was doing my thing all over the globe; and Paul's regular work, installing computers, and his work for the Reapers, soliciting funds,

100

recruiting new members, kept him constantly on the move. But when we could be together, there wasn't anyone else for either of us."

"And the child, Milly?"

"No better, no worse, year after year. A bright friendly four year old who was growing into a lovely girl and then woman, physically. Paul had found a couple named Welch who became foster parents to Milly. He paid all her expenses and, I guess, kicked in a bonus for the Welches. It seemed like a happy arrangement."

"The Reapers," Quist persisted.

"When I came back from touring Europe with Ossie's group I found Paul caught up in tensions that weren't usual with him. After we'd enjoyed the happiness of being together again for a few days he told me what it was. The FBI was working on what he called a 'scam,' to get him and the Reapers. He was pretty certain agents had infiltrated the organization in the hope of exposing drug trafficking, manipulating funds, private immoralities—which could mean Paul and me in their eyes—and acts of violence committed by some of the dedicated members. It was a technique that angered Paul—moving in, inciting to crime, and then lowering the boom. 'It is a technique the late J. Edgar Hoover loved,' Paul told me. 'Teasing someone into committing a crime and then making an arrest.' He thought we should play it cool for a while, not be seen together in public, not be trapped together in private. He hoped to be able to expose the infiltrators and then things could get back to normal. And then—it happened!"

Quist waited. Whatever was coming was almost too much for her.

"Paul came to my hotel in the early hours of a morning— four, five o'clock—a man I didn't know, cold, hard, caught up in a terrible rage. He had come to say good-bye to me, forever. He was going to kill a man and pay the penalty for it if he had to. I must never tell anyone why—and I never have until now."

"It can't hurt Paul, baby," Ossie said. "He's gone."

"You have to remember that Milly was now twenty-two, a beautiful child-woman, living with the Welch family. It seems that Mrs. Welch left Milly alone in their apartment that afternoon to keep a dentist appointment and do some shopping. She was gone for about three hours. It was perfectly usual for Milly to be left alone. When Mrs. Welch got home she found Milly, huddled in a corner of her room, stark naked, covered with bloody scratches and wounds, in shock. It took Mrs. Welch only minutes to realize that Milly had been raped and beaten."

"Oh, brother!" Ossie said.

"Anyone else might have called the police, but Mrs. Welch knew Paul might have trouble with the police, so she managed to get in touch with him. Milly was unable to tell him anything. Paul had a gift for drawing caricatures of people. He suspected the villain must be someone out to get him, gone to investigate the child, and—and violated her. He drew pictures for Mildred until she suddenly reacted to one in terror. That was enough for him.

"I pleaded with him to go to the police. He wouldn't. If that helpless girl was brought into court, she couldn't really testify and make it stick. The rest of her miserable life people would gape at her—a poor idiot who had to let herself be had." Dyanne drew a deep, shuddering breath. "Just after nine o'clock that morning Paul walked into the offices of Francis O'Brien, attorney, and shot the man dead."

"He was the rapist?" Quist asked.

"Paul certainly believed he was."

"Pretty slim evidence. The reaction of a shell-shocked, autistic child to a caricature."

"It was enough for Paul."

"It was never brought up in court, in the trial?"

Dyanne shook her head. "I was the only person who knew. It wouldn't have helped Paul if I'd broken my promise to him. He had committed a murder, whatever the motive."

"Mrs. Welch? She didn't come forward?"

"I don't think she guessed the truth. There was a scam. O'Brien was part of it. Like everyone else, I suppose she thought that was the motive. She loves Milly. She's kept the horror story to herself."

"It wouldn't do any good to tell it now, would it?" Ossie asked.

Quist was reaching for straws in his mind. "The Reapers think Paul killed O'Brien because O'Brien was trying to destroy them through the scam. The judge and Zorn are part of the System that set up the scam. If they knew that wasn't the reason for Paul's action—"

"You don't know them, Mr. Quist. What happened to Milly would be a far greater crime to them than the scam," Dyanne said. "They might very well up the ante. Sexual universality is unforgivable."

"How can they be turned off?" Quist asked, not really expecting an answer.

"I wish I could tell you, Mr. Quist," Dyanne said.

"Names!" Quist said, sounding desperate. "You must know some names in the Reaper membership. Paul was at the top!"

She gave him a bitter smile. "Smith, Jones, and Brown," she said. "Surely the FBI, from their scam operation, can give you names."

3 Three o'clock in the afternoon. Half a day gone and Quist hadn't advanced himself an inch in an effort to find himself a weapon to use against the Reapers. The judge had produced nothing, Martin Wilshire, the lawyer, had produced nothing, and Dyanne Jordan had added only a grim page to the tragic history of the late Paul Kramer.

From the lobby of the Beaumont, Quist called the Complex. Captain Haller was back at the telephone in Dan Garvey's office. There had been a contact with Smith in the Cup.

"More stalling," Haller reported. "He will call back at six o'clock. He hopes, for my sake, I'll have something to offer by then. He tells me he is 'beginning to get bored.' You, Mr. Quist?"

"I've been trying to get names that could lead us to a Judas," Quist said. "Nothing from the judge and nothing from Wilshire. I got a lead to Paul Kramer's girl friend. I've just left her. No names, but she suggests the FBI as a source."

"We've been there," Haller said. "They have names that came out of a scam they were staging. Maybe half a dozen they think were real names. My men in the city, Akleman and O'Neil, haven't been able to locate any of them, gone underground, disappeared."

"There must be hundreds of them, thousands of them, across the country!"

"Shut up like unsteamed clams," Haller said. "The old name, rank, and serial number routine. 'My name is Brown!' A couple of dozen Browns so far. It seems Brown is a foot soldier, not an officer."

"I'll be out there before the six o'clock call," Quist said. "One thing that might be useful. The girl who was in your office out there early on, the singer, Sally Craven? It seems that the man who plays piano for her, Pete Damon—he's supposedly one of the hostages—is, or once was, a Reaper. It occurs to me that Craven broad might have been Smith's source of information about who was where that first hour."

"So you haven't wasted your time entirely, Quist," Haller said. He sounded pleased. "That could be the first handle we've had to anything."

Quist called his office. Connie Parmalee was back on the job. The judge's files had produced nothing that seemed to have any value to her.

"Fascinating reading," she said, "but zip, nothing, as far as anything useful is concerned. Mark Kreevich has been trying to reach you. If you got in touch by three o'clock, you're to call him. He used the word *urgent*. You might still catch him. It's only ten after three."

Luck for once.

"I was just leaving," Kreevich said. "We think we've located Carl Zorn."

"Where?"

"A cottage—about forty miles up the line in Darien."

"Does he explain why he hasn't been in touch?"

"He doesn't explain anything because we haven't been able to reach him directly," Kreevich said. "Phone off the hook. I'm headed up there. I thought you might be helpful. With Lydia a hostage he might be willing to talk to you."

"How do you know he's there if you can't reach him?"

"Local police. He's there—and asking for special protection from them. He tells them he anticipates a visit from Lefty Orso. Where are you?"

"Hotel Beaumont."

"I'll meet you outside the front entrance in ten minutes, traffic permitting."

"I want to be back on the Island by six. There's to be another contact with Smith."

"You want help, don't you?"

They were lucky getting out of the city well ahead of the heavy home-bound commuter traffic. Quist relayed what he had to his friend. Kreevich, working another angle on the situation, hadn't had much more success than Quist.

"Orso has moved me over, officially," the detective explained. "My job is to protect the judge and Zorn from him and his goons. Oh, not to deploy bodyguards. But a homicide has been threatened. For once I'm ordered to prevent a crime, not solve it after it's happened. We've got undercover cops watching Orso's business affairs all the time—the waterfront, the drug business, loan sharking. The sonofabitch is a multimillionaire, you know? And where is he? Sitting in the sun on his private beach down on the Jersey coast, laughing at us and letting us see the hair on his chest! Always the perfect alibi for Luigi Orso in person. A hundred guns ready to do whatever he orders anywhere on the map of the whole stinking globe! I wouldn't want you to quote me to the commissioner, chum, but if Orso makes up his mind to have Judge Padgett and Carl Zorn rubbed out, I don't think he can be stopped. At the exact moment the shots are fired, Luigi Orso will be sitting on his beach in the sun, smoking a big Cuban cigar, and laughing at the cops we have watching him. Alibi Ike in person!"

"Protective custody for the judge and Zorn?" Quist suggested.

"For life?" Kreevich made a growling sound. "Our best chance is to persuade Orso that we're making some sort of headway with Smith, get him to hold off while we try to make a deal."

"Surely he won't want to get involved with murders he's publicly threatened to commit," Quist said.

"What holds the world together?" Kreevich asked, his voice bitter. "Orso's empire is held together because he 'takes care' of his people. That's why he made a public threat. So that everyone would know that Pappa Luigi takes care of his people. If we don't get his guys and their broads out of the Cup in a hurry, he'll have to carry through."

"And you can't stop him?"

"I didn't say I couldn't arrest the hit men, or build up a good enough case against Orso so that the D.A. can put him out of business for a stretch. Stop them from killing Judge Padgett and Zorn? I don't like to bet against myself, but I don't like the odds."

They raced up the Connecticut highway toward Darien, paying no attention to the speed laws. They were in an unmarked police car, but highway cops had been warned of their approach and ignored them or gave them a wave of the hand as they shot past. In the center of the town of Darien a local trooper was waiting for them. It was explained to them that Zorn's place was on a point of land in Tokeneke, a rich, almost suburban community.

"Right on the water—Long Island Sound," the trooper explained. "Only one way to get to it by land, and we've got every inch of that covered. Zorn knows you're coming, Lieutenant. Follow me."

Under other circumstances Quist might not have thought of Zorn's place as a "fortress." A rocky arm of land reached out into the Sound, not more than fifty yards wide and perhaps a couple of hundred yards long. The house, stone and stucco and painted a Spanish pink, perched on the very end, overlooking water on three sides of it, fifty or sixty feet above the water level. The only easy access to the house was the blue stone driveway that led in from the mainland and this, when they arrived, was blocked by police cars and men, armed with rifles, patrolling either side of it.

The house, when they reached it, was fascinatingly different. You drove straight into a three-car garage. Off the garage was a large playroom with a ping-pong table, a circular card table with poker chips in racks ready for the players, a bar in one corner, a glassed-in cabinet for guns, but with no guns in sight when Quist and Kreevich were led in by a local trooper. You went down a flight of stairs, below the road level but still high above the Sound, to an attractive, sun-flooded living room, a kitchen and a master bedroom and bath adjoining it. Another flight down, Quist learned later, were four guest bedrooms and baths. At that level there was a wide balcony built out over the water, and an iron stairway leading down to a boat dock.

They found Carl Zorn in the living room on the second level. There were two uniformed troopers and two men in summer sports clothes positioned at the windows on three sides of the room. Quist guessed the men in sports clothes were Zorn's private bodyguards. On a stretcher table in the center of the room was a collection of rifles, shotguns, and Quist saw at least two machine pistols, evidently brought down from their accustomed place in the game room. There were boxes of ammunition. It was a small arsenal.

Quist at that moment was more interested in the man who had convicted Paul Kramer and sent him to his eventual self-destruction in prison. Carl Zorn was a tall, athletically built man about forty. Dark hair was crew cut; the summer sun had tanned him a deep brown; bright black eyes were never still; a thin slit of a mouth suggested some sort of inner cruelty. Quist didn't like him from the first moment he laid eyes on him.

"You're out of your bailiwick here, aren't you, Lieutenant?" Zorn asked Kreevich. He had a strong voice, a courtroom voice.

"The commissioner thinks of you as someone under his protection," Kreevich said. He gestured toward the gun-ladened table. "You afraid of attack?"

"Only a macho idiot wouldn't be afraid if he was threatened by two power groups—the Reapers and Lefty Orso and his gangster army. I intend to stay alive, Kreevich, and this looks like the best place to make my stand."

Kreevich wandered over to one of the windows. "No way to approach you by water—in the daylight," he said. "What happens after dark?"

"Floodlights and a couple of searchlights. They were installed in a happier time when swimming at night was a safe recreation." Zorn turned to Quist. "I understand you're Julian Quist? I understand some broad you were wining and dining is one of the hostages at the Cup."

"The 'broad,'" Quist said, his voice cold, "is Miss Lydia Morton. She and I have been living together for a good many years. She is everything, perhaps more, that a wife could be to me."

"Sorry," Zorn said. "The television report didn't go into your private life. It just said a lady you'd been dining with was being held."

"I like *lady* better than *broad*," Quist said.

"Listen, Quist, when you're facing death you couldn't give a damn what word happens to pop up first. You and Kreevich didn't come out here to give me a lesson in manners. Why have you come?"

"To try to save your life and three hundred and twenty-seven others," Kreevich said.

"I understand one of the hostages had been released. That leaves three hundred and twenty-six."

"There is also Judge Padgett. Do you remember him,

109

Zorn? And there are fifty-two Reapers who may be crazy enough to blow themselves up."

"*Crazy* is too mild a word," Zorn said. He glanced at a gold wristwatch. "I understand from the TV there is to be a new contact with Captain Haller at six o'clock—an hour and forty minutes. You didn't come out here to gossip."

"You made a study of those people—the Reapers," Kreevich said. "I could have asked you what I need to know on the telephone if you'd had it on the hook."

"Seems like everyone in the world was trying to reach me on the phone—neighbors, people I never heard of, reporters, politicians who wanted to look as if they were trying to help. I gave up. I had to get ready for whatever may be coming. So what would you have asked me on the phone?"

"For names," Kreevich said. "Names in the Reapers' membership, preferably people running the show."

Zorn's laugh was short. "You've come up with the Smith-Jones-Brown syndrome?"

"Captain Haller believes, and I believe, that somewhere in the organization is someone who can be bought," Kreevich said. "A Judas. If we could fix on such a man and broadcast his betrayal of the Reapers' goals and aims, it's possible those people in the Cup might settle for a lot less."

"By six o'clock?"

"Haller hopes he can stall for more time, but we need to move fast."

Zorn's eyes narrowed to two glittering slits. "Haller hopes!" he said. His eyes swiveled to Quist. "I don't like to say this in front of you, Quist, but I'm a hell of a lot more deeply concerned with my survival than I am for the survival of three hundred and twenty-six, or three hundred and seventy-eight, or whatever it is out there in the Cup. You ought to understand that, because you'll have to admit you care first and only for Miss Morton's safety, and to hell with the rest of us."

"But winning the ball game produces the same happy result for everyone," Kreevich said, before Quist could answer. "The way I see it we have an organization of several thousand young people spread out across the country, really believing in some kind of whacky religious cult, in the hands of a few leaders who raise God knows how much money, skim off the cream, and leave what's left to enforce 'God's Justice.' Now, who are the cream eaters? Because they are almost certain to be phonies—at least from the point of view of their dedicated followers."

"Would you believe I spent months trying to come up with that answer?" Zorn said. "I was trying to get everything in the world I could on Paul Kramer. You know what I came up with? Smith, Jones, and Brown—interchangeable histories, interchangeable records. You haven't got time to try that all over again, Lieutenant."

"What about the FBI?" Quist asked. "They were working a scam on the Reapers. They knew Kramer's real name. They must have come up with others."

"Francis O'Brien ran that scam," Zorn said. "If he kept records, we couldn't come up with them after Kramer shot him."

"Surely he wasn't working the scam alone," Kreevich said. "There were technicians who tapped phones, made tape recordings. The FBI doesn't run one-man scams. There has to be a witness to what happens, and a witness to the witness!"

Zorn nodded. "Let me tell you," he said. "What I got from the FBI was that O'Brien's scam wasn't working very well. Their target was Kramer. They hoped to get from him the names of those cream skimmers you mentioned, the source of the drugs that almost all the Reapers use, the sources of firearms and explosives that the Reapers buy in quantities large enough to equip a small army. They were offering Kramer deals in drugs and weapons whereby he could skim the cream off the cream! Kramer was playing hard to get, they told me. Maybe he committed himself to O'Brien, guessed the truth before O'Brien could report to his superiors, went to O'Brien's office, and shot him dead."

Quist could feel his teeth grinding together. He knew the truth about that from Dyanne Jordan.

"But no other real names came out?"

"Smith, Jones, and Brown," Zorn said.

One of the bodyguards spoke up, sharply. "Boat at two o'clock," he said.

Zorn didn't seem to be in any great hurry. He picked up a pair of field glasses from the weapons table and went over to the window. He focused on a small power launch cruising some distance from shore.

"Rubbernecking," he said, lowering the glasses. "The McCormacks. They have a summer house just down the beach. They probably wonder what's cooking." He turned back to Kreevich. "I'm not a television fan," he said. "The Reapers took over the Stirrup Cup just before midnight, right? Their demands were being broadcast very shortly after that, right? Out here we didn't know anything had happened till breakfast time."

"No one tried to phone you—to warn you?" Kreevich asked.

"I had the damn thing disconnected so I could get some sleep," Zorn said. "When I heard the news and tried to make an out-call, everybody in God's world was trying to call me. I left it off the hook—jack's pulled out. Let 'em get a busy signal. But I've done some pretty fancy thinking since then."

"Like?"

"It's no secret that Luigi Orso controls most of the drug traffic on the East Coast. He supplies the Reapers, or he gets paid by someone he allows to supply them. I've been waiting, Lieutenant."

"For what?"

"For Orso's three men and their three girls to be released from the Cup. There was no way for Orso to contact the Smith in charge, so he made a grandstand play."

"Threatening to deliver you and the judge—dead?"

Zorn nodded. "It may have been his way of letting them know they had three of his people and their women, accidentally caught in the Cup when they were having a night at the races. Harm Luigi's people and they'd know their supply of coke would dry up overnight. He knew his threat would be broadcast and Smith would hear it."

"If you're right, then you're safe," Kreevich said.

"If I'm right, safe from Orso," Zorn said, "but not from the Reapers, and not from the families and friends of three hundred-odd hostages if they're not released. Those people are going to think Padgett and I should give ourselves up!"

"The judge suggested he might do just that," Quist said.

"The judge is an old man and a damn fool," Zorn said. "He may not care whether he lives any longer, but I do and I mean to."

"Round and round," Kreevich said. "What are the Reapers' routines? They profess to be a religious-oriented group. Where do they meet? Who preaches 'the word,' whatever it is?"

"Smith preaches the word," Zorn said. "Jones passes the plate. Brown puts in his tithe and whatever contributions he's been able to collect. And I suspect, as you do, that most of what Brown puts in the plate goes right back to Jones and Smith."

113

"Whoever they are."

Zorn's smile was mocking. "Oh, well, there are the Smith and Jones who hold meetings in an abandoned tenement in Harlem—and the Smith and Jones who hold street-corner meetings in Brooklyn—and the Smiths and Joneses who preside at meetings in Chicago, and New Orleans, and Kansas City, and Hollywood. Names? There was a routine when I was working on the Kramer case. 'What's your name?' 'Brown.' 'And what's your name?' 'Brown.' 'You two brothers?' 'Yes, sir. Brothers in the Reapers and in the Truth as taught by Simeon Taylor.' All brothers, all Browns or Smiths or Joneses."

"And these people are all terrorists?" Quist asked.

"Certainly not all of them fire a gun, or wield a knife, or garrote people with bailing wire, or burn them alive in a gasoline-soaked house, or plant bombs in the starting mechanisms of automobiles, or hang men from a cotton-wood tree in Texas." Zorn's voice rose, the prosecutor addressing the jury. "Not all of them do those things, but all of them say 'amen'—or whatever a Reaper says. All of them contribute to a kitty that buys the tools for terror. Nobody talks."

"Somewhere in an organization of that size there has to be a weak link—weak links, for God's sake," Kreevich said.

"This much I learned during the Kramer business," Zorn said. "The penalty for betraying the cause, the cult, what have you, is death. No reprieve, no appeal. We felt Kramer must have thought he'd talked too much to O'Brien in the scam. That's why he murdered openly, let himself be arrested, offered no real defense. He let the law convict him, but the law couldn't kill him—so he killed himself. That's why you're looking for a needle in a haystack, Lieutenant. I doubt if there is a Reaper anywhere who will risk playing Judas for you. The Reapers know something

114

the average American doesn't—the deterrent value in a no-appeal death penalty."

A trooper came down the stairway from the upper level.

"Came over my car radio, Mr. Zorn. Captain Haller at the Island Complex is trying to reach Lieutenant Kreevich or Mr. Quist. It's urgent, they say."

Quist glanced at his watch. It was a quarter past five—forty-five minutes till contact with the Smith in the Stirrup Cup.

Zorn plugged in a telephone to a jack connection in the baseboard. Kreevich dialed the special number at the Complex. Haller himself answered.

"Lieutenant Kreevich here, Captain."

"Glad I got through to you, Lieutenant. You with Zorn?"

"Yes."

"Mr. Quist with you?"

"Yes."

"We've had some action here," Haller said, in his calm voice. "Freight elevator in the Cup surfaced from the basement. Iron trash barrels. One of them contained a body."

"Oh, brother!"

"Tell Mr. Quist it's a man. His name is Johnny Lupo, a kitchen helper. Possibly he's the one Smith told us was hurt when the Reapers first took over. Police doctor says he died of a skull fracture. But sending him out is a message of some sort, I suspect. Have you and Quist come up with anything useful at all? We've got to bargain in about forty minutes."

"Smith, Jones, and Brown," Kreevich said.

"My two men in New York—Akleman and O'Neil—the same. The whole damned cult seems to have gone underground. What about the situation where you are?"

"Zorn is well protected," Kreevich said. "House like a

fort, weapons, state police, personal bodyguards. Safe for now, for tonight, for tomorrow—but for how long after that?"

"Will he move from there?"

"Seemed like a waste of time to ask him," Kreevich said. "He's a man who trusts himself ahead of anyone else."

"So keep your fingers crossed, Lieutenant," Haller said. "If Smith starts sending out bodies, we're going to have to act, no matter what the risk."

"And my toes."

"How's that, Lieutenant?"

"Crossed—like my fingers," Kreevich said.

About a year ago, Dan Garvey remembered, hijackers had taken over a plane in Pakistan and held over a hundred people hostage for more than thirteen days—the longest such hostage-holding in history—at least up to that point. One hostage had been shot and his body thrown out of the plane as a warning. In the end authorities gave in to the hijackers' demands—the release of fifty-odd political prisoners. "We will not deal with terrorists," the government had said. In the end they had to deal because they believed after days of negotiations that the hijackers would do exactly what they threatened to do.

Having spent a whole day and half a night with Haller, Vic Lorch, Captain Jansen of the state police, and a parade of experts from the police, the FBI, the army, Garvey had gradually let himself be convinced that Smith, the voice from the Cup, was fanatical enough to do exactly what *he* threatened to do. There was a grim difference between Smith's demands and the demands of those Pakistani hijackers. You might regret turning loose prisoners you considered to be criminals deserving their punishment, but to save a hundred or more innocent lives you would, in the end, do it. Turning over two innocent men, decent, honest public servants, to be executed by fanatics in order to save over three hundred innocent hostages was an entirely different ball game. It couldn't be done. There were no imaginable circumstances under which it could be done. None of the experts who came and went from Garvey's office, now Haller's headquarters, even mentioned the possibility.

In the long run there was only one course of action that could be taken. A careful plan must be devised for storming the Cup, a plan for getting to the man with the detonator before he could blow them all to bits, and taking their chances with fifty or more other armed lunatics. Would those fifty fight the invaders, or would they turn their weapons on the hostages and then themselves? They were, Garvey thought, far enough "out" to do just that. The death toll on all sides could be horrifying.

What else? One thing was clear, a consensus opinion of all the experts. An attack with even a small chance of surprise and success could only take place after dark. Reapers, stationed at key spots inside the Cup, could see any massing, or approach of an attack force in the daytime, even before invaders could get within yards of the building. Haller would have to stall Smith until darkness came, which would be about eight-thirty or a quarter to nine, daylight saving time. A six o'clock talk—and pray for time, Garvey thought.

The plan for attack had been taking shape all day. Army troops and special police were bivouacked about a mile from the Complex, out of sight. The main problem was the press. Reporters were briefed, pledged to withhold the release of any story about the presence of troops. Maybe they would all be good little boys and girls, but there was no way to be sure that someone living in the area, snooping around outside the grounds, wouldn't spread the word. Every time the radio and television set in the office came on with a newscast on the situation, Garvey held his breath. No mention of troops so far.

One of the first things suggested by some genius was the possibility of getting into the Cup by way of the roof. Men could be lowered from a helicopter.

"Which could be heard inside the Cup long before men could be lowered," Haller pointed out.

The "genius" came up with a plan. They should start flying a steady chopper patrol over the building now, so that the steady sound of engines would become a part of the scene. Since midafternoon police choppers had circled the Cup. The noise was perpetual. After dark it would be continuous, but they hoped not alarming to the Reapers. If they would wait till dark!

After dark the Complex would be without lights of any sort. All racing and any other events were shut down, the public barred. In the darkness men would take their positions, so that at a given signal, every door and every window at ground level would come under attack.

"Killing God knows how many of the people we're trying to save," Captain Haller said. Negotiating was his business. He still hoped there was a way to persuade Smith to sit tight. "Tomorrow night will be as good as tonight—and we could arrive at something with Smith before that."

The consensus of the army, the troopers, the police, and Vic Lorch and his security people was that waiting was too big a risk to run. It should be tonight.

"One shot gets fired and that man with the detonator can blow up the place before one man gets inside," Haller insisted.

Experts, along with Garvey, poured over the blueprints of the building. Mike Romano, the manager of the Cup, who had been turned loose at the time of the seizure of the building, after being shown where explosives were planted and where the detonator was, sat in on the discussion.

118

There were two windows to the office, blocked out now by drawn venetian blinds.

"They showed me the guy sitting there, his hand held over the plunger to that detonator," Mike told them.

"So he's been sitting there now for what—sixteen, seventeen hours?" Vic Lorch asked.

"Not necessarily the same guy," someone said.

"And not with his hand held out over the plunger," Lorch said. "It would drop off if he kept holding it out there in space—his arm." He looked around at the others. "By now, he's just sitting there. He hears a threatening sound and in two seconds he can raise his arm in position to blow up the joint. but that two seconds is our one chance."

The room was silent, waiting for him to go on.

"We don't move everybody in close—just one man to one of those windows to the office. That man has a hand grenade and he smashes the window and lets fly! If there's any luck coming our way the man inside never gets his hand up to push down the plunger. Then we attack all points and hope!"

"And if, as you say, we get lucky we won't lose more than half the hostages," Haller said.

"Better than losing them all," Lorch said.

Garvey thought of Lydia and felt his stomach muscles tighten. The hostages who died in the attack wouldn't be chosen or selected for death. It would just be a question of whether they were in the line of fire when an attack took place. Garvey, a man of action himself, approved Lorch's plan, but suddenly he wanted Haller to have another chance.

"Who attacks that office with a grenade?" someone asked.

"Should be a volunteer, someone who's handled grenades and can pull the pin at exactly the right moment—a soldier, a cop, one of my boys."

"Let me see what I can do," Haller said. "It's twenty minutes to six. You can wait that long before you make a decision."

There wasn't a choice to make. There was no way a volunteer, armed with a grenade, could get to the office window in daylight. Haller had his six o'clock chance, experts not withstanding.

As the electric clock moved to within seconds of six, the office became deathly still. Haller lifted the receiver and the dial tone, coming through the squawk box, sounded like a buzz saw.

"Good evening, Captain Haller. It's nice to deal with someone so prompt." It was Smith's mocking voice. "I'm sorry we had to send you a dead man. We're rather crowded in here, you know."

"Why was he killed?" Haller asked.

"I told you the first time we talked that one of the kitchen workers had attacked one of my people. There was a retaliation, of course. I had hoped our hostage doctor would be able to save him, but the injury was too severe and our facilities in here too limited. I regret any loss of life unless it is for the just payment of a debt. Which brings me to the purpose of your call, Captain."

"You know you're asking more than I can get authority to deliver," Haller said.

"I know you keep saying that, Captain. I listen to the radio and watch the television screen and I hear and see wise men, and politicians, and great legal minds, and, laughably, ministers of the Gospel who clearly cannot read or understand their own Bible. 'As ye sow, so shall ye reap.' 'An eye for an eye, a tooth for a tooth.'"

"We could arrive at a ransom figure," Haller said. "We could add immunity from prosecution, transportation to any place in the world you choose."

"You know places that would take us, Captain?" Smith

asked. He chuckled. "Broadhurst offered half a million for his wife, you recall. The same price for everyone would bring the ransom to about a hundred and sixty million dollars. Are you thinking in those terms, Captain? After all, Ronnie Hood and his merry men in the White House knock that much off programs for the poor every day in the week. Surely they could afford half a million a head for their rich supporters in here."

"If you're interested in talking money it can be discussed," Haller said.

"I'm not interested, Captain!" The laughter had gone from Smith's voice and it was harsh. "I am giving you time for you and all the wise men to let the situation soak in. There is just one price for the hostages. I repeat it. Judge Steven Padgett and Prosecutor Carl Zorn in our hands to be dealt with in our way. There is no use talking about any other price. There *is* no other price. Think about it, Captain. See to it that everyone else in authority thinks about it. I will give you till nine o'clock tomorrow morning to say yes or no. If it is no, I will begin to send out bodies in the trash, as I promised. It seems a pity that people will have to die to convince you that you have no options." There was a moment of silence, almost unbearable. "Is Mr. Quist there?" Smith asked.

"No."

"Too bad," Smith said. "I have Miss Morton here to speak to him."

"I'll speak to her!" Dan Garvey shouted, ignoring Haller's rules. "I'm Quist's partner, Miss Morton's friend."

"It's Garvey, isn't it?" Smith said. "Well, perhaps, for a moment."

"Lydia!" Garvey called out.

"Hi, Dan." Her voice was calm, controlled. "Julian is all right?"

"He's fine. We talked to him not long ago. He'll flip his wig when he knows he might have talked to you."

121

"There isn't much to talk about, Dan," Lydia said, "except to say that I think Mr. Smith means what he says and will do what he says."

Garvey realized she must have promised to say that. That's why she was on.

"Are you all right—physically?" Garvey asked. "Has anyone tried to harm you?"

"I'm better off than some," she said. "I'm not hysterical. Tell Julian I love him."

"I will!"

"So much for personal messages," Smith's voice broke in. "And now a few words for your professional ear, Captain Haller."

"I'm here," Haller said.

"I think I know exactly how your mind is working, and all the masterminds surrounding you. You think you cannot meet our demand—two for three hundred and twenty-five. It would be more moral, you think, to save two men than three hundred and twenty-five innocents. You would prefer, for example, to have Miss Morton's blood on your conscience than the blood of a doddering old judge and a two-penny prosecutor. Are you listening, Captain?"

"Yes."

"I've been trying to guess how I would be thinking in your position, Captain. For example, those choppers that have been flying over the building for the last few hours. We are supposed to think they are part of your technique of containment. Right? I suspect, however, that you have other plans for them. You will be hoping that we will become so accustomed to them that when, after dark, one of them flies low we will ignore it. You will drop a man or men on the roof and try to get at us that way. Is that a good guess or not, Captain?"

Haller didn't speak. The men in the office stared at each other. Dan Garvey's lips moved in silent profanity.

"The second thing I would do, Captain," Smith continued, mockery back in his voice, "would be to find a way to immobilize the man who controls the explosives we have planted in here. Mike Romano, the manager, has told you where he is—sitting in Romano's office, his hand on a detonator. Let's see, what would I do if I were in your shoes? I think I would arm a man with a hand grenade and have him sneak up to one of the office windows after dark. He would heave his grenade into the office and hope our man would be caught off base. It might work, you know, except for one thing. Are you listening, Captain?"

"I'm listening," Haller said. He sounded like a ghost of himself.

"The reason it won't work, Captain, is that I have moved my man and the detonator out of Romano's office. To where? That you will have to guess, Captain. How close am I?"

No answer from Haller.

"Finally, if I were you, Captain, I would have a small army waiting somewhere out of sight from these windows. After dark they will move in close. The moment your grenadier sets off his little bomb in an empty office, they will charge all the doors and windows on the ground level. When the first shot is fired to smash a lock or break a windowpane, my people, armed with machine pistols, will open fire on the hostages, all gathered in one place. You won't have a man in the building before most of them are dead. So, I suggest you begin rethinking the whole problem, Captain. I'll talk to you at nine in the morning. I hope by then you will have decided that the judge and Zorn are not worth the price you'll have to pay."

Dial tone.

"The sonofabitch is right down the main street with it," Garvey almost shouted. "Now what?"

Part Three

1 The perfect and hopeless stalemate, Quist thought. He and Kreevich were headed back down the Connecticut highway to New York. They had left Carl Zorn in his fortress, surrounded by armed police, with his own bodyguards and weapons, waiting for an attack to come from somewhere. The Reapers? Orso? Even his own world, which might suddenly decide to trade him for the hostages? He might be a hostile, aggressive, vulgar bastard, but in any civilized world his life wasn't tradeable.

A little after six, when they were fifteen miles underway, Quist had called the Complex from the telephone on Kreevich's police car. The connection wasn't perfect, but Dan Garvey laid it out for Quist. The Reapers were not amateurs at terror. Smith had anticipated every step of a careful plan. There was no way to storm in and save, at best, more than a handful of the three hundred and more hostages. There was no way to make a deal. Neither Quist, nor Kreevich, nor Haller's special cops had come up with any lead to a Judas who might provide them with any sort of information with which to negotiate. Smith, Jones, and Brown!

"How had you seen this Judas thing working?" Kreevich asked. He had driven for a mile or so in silence after Quist had relayed the news from the Complex.

"Someone willing to talk," Quist said. "Someone Smith's army in the Cup would know was real. Information from that someone that might make Smith's soldiers doubt the purpose of the whole adventure at the Cup. If we could show them that money was the real object of Smith's campaign, and not the Reapers' so-called moral cause—"

"That's asking for a hell of a lot to find in a few hours," Kreevich said. "How would you get the word to them if you found what you're looking for?"

"Television," Quist said. "They must be watching it round the clock."

"So you find someone who knows something. Long shot. You persuade that someone to betray his leaders. How?"

"Money."

"Negotiate with him? We can grow old negotiating."

"Maybe there is someone who is a genuine believer in what Simeon Taylor, the founder, stood for. Maybe that person would believe in mass violence for the cause, but not just to make dishonest Smiths rich."

"No way—not in any time that we have available," Kreevich said. "It takes a man a lot of time to decide to betray his friends." He laughed, a bitter little sound. "You could write a script, hire an actor to deliver the lines and pray that someone would believe him."

"It has to be someone some of them would know. I have a feeling that Smith in the Cup would smell out a fake with the first word. He's probably guessing right now that we're thinking along those lines."

"Wilshire, the lawyer, would he fake it out?" Kreevich suggested. "We could certainly raise enough money to make it worth his while."

"It would have to be a lot of money," Quist said. "Turning in clients could be the end of his legal career."

"Saving three hundred and twenty-five lives would make him a hero," Kreevich said.

Quist didn't answer. He could feel all his muscles tightening as he stared straight ahead along the highway. An actor who would be believed? There was such a person, certainly known to all of them by sight, one of them, indirectly, who could know a thousand secrets! If he could persuade Dyanne Jordan to help, they just might pull it off.

He picked up the car phone and dialed the Complex number again. "I've come up with a far-out chance, Dan," he told Garvey when he got him. "I'll need you. You can make it in to the Hotel Beaumont in less than an hour."

"So?"

"I'll meet you there in the Trapeze Bar. Meet you, or call you there."

"This isn't just fun and games?"

"Have you forgotten, friend? Lydia's out there under the gun. Please call Connie and tell her I'll need her to stand by. And if you can find Rusty Grimes, the *Newsview* man, bring him with you. Tell him I might have the scoop of all time for him." Quist put down the phone and glanced at Kreevich. "In the days before Lydia became the best part of my life I had pretty good luck with women. Pray that I've got some charm left over somewhere, will you, Mark?"

Quist knew that charm in the accepted man-woman sense was not what he was going to need. He was going to need a very special magic to enlist the help of the beautiful woman in Suite 1411 at the Beaumont. He was tempted to find an ally, possibly Ossie Lord, possibly his rather special friend, the manager of the Beaumont, Pierre Chambrun, a wise man with a flare for the bizarre. But involving anyone else meant taking time to explain and convince, with every passing minute like a time-bomb ticking away with no knowledge of when it might go off and with Lydia's life thrown away if it all took too long.

It was a soft summer evening, still daylight, when Quist reached the Beaumont at about seven-thirty. A little more than twelve hours to go—if Smith kept his word. It could take hours to set what Quist had in mind into motion; hours *after* he had persuaded Dyanne Jordan to play along with him. *If* he persuaded her!

Watters, the front doorman at the Beaumont, was a nodding acquaintance and the occasional recipient of a generous tip when he had gotten Quist a taxi on a rainy night. He was eager to talk about the siege at the Cup, properly sympathetic about Miss Morton, and more important, willing to help. Quist wanted to avoid the lobby crowd at dinner time. There would be too many people who knew him by sight and would delay him with questions. Watters took him around to a service entrance on the side street and got him to a freight elevator that would take him up to fourteen without anyone seeing him.

At fourteen he found his way out into the public corridor and to the door of 1411. He rang the doorbell and waited. She could be gone somewhere—for dinner, or perhaps even to fulfill a singing engagement. It wasn't until he pressed the bell that it occurred to him she might not be there when he needed her.

The door opened and she faced him, wearing a dark lavender housecoat. Her handsome face clouded when she saw him.

"I thought you were the room-service waiter," she said. "I'd ordered myself some supper."

In the background Quist could hear the television set going. "You know that nothing has happened," he said.

"I'm sorry for you, Mr. Quist," she said. "I know what it's like to have someone you love in danger."

"Please let me talk to you," he said.

She hesitated a moment and then opened the door wider. "I've told you everything I know to tell you, Mr. Quist."

"I need help," he said. "If you wanted to give it you could."

Her dark, expressive eyes widened. "I don't know any way to help you."

"I'll tell you if you'll let me."

130

He caught a glimpse of himself in the foyer mirror as he followed her in. The pallor of his face startled him. He looked like a stranger to himself.

Dyanne switched off the television set and stood by it, waiting for him to say what he had to say.

"If you've been listening to the reports on your set," he said, "you know that we've been given a final deadline—tomorrow morning at nine."

She nodded. "That, and a plea from the governor to the Reapers to accept some other solution than senseless slaughter."

"That I hadn't heard, but neither the governor nor the president himself is going to be able to move them. You might."

She opened her mouth, but no sound came.

"May I sit down, Dyanne? May I call you Dyanne? I've been on the go for nearly twenty-four hours. I feel as if my legs wouldn't hold me up."

She gestured to an upholstered armchair and he sat down, pressing the palms of his hands against his eyes for a moment. He hadn't realized how close to exhaustion he was. He and Lydia had gone to the Stirrup for dinner just twenty-four hours ago. It seemed like years.

"I have some brandy—if it would help," Dyanne said.

"It just might save my life," Quist said.

She went to the sideboard and poured brandy into a liqueur glass. She brought it to him. It felt like a warming fire as he sipped it, gratefully.

The doorbell rang. It was the room-service waiter with Dyanne's supper on a little wagon.

"Can I order something for you?" she asked Quist.

He shook his head.

"There are cups in the cabinet over there, madam," the waiter said. "If your guest would like to share your coffee—?"

131

"Thank you." She signed for the dinner, obviously writing in a generous tip. The waiter was all smiles as he left. She made no move to touch what had been brought her. When the suite door closed she spoke. "You said I—I might persuade the Reapers to—what?"

Quist turned his head from side to side to loosen the tensions at the back of his neck. "We've had a theory, almost from the beginning," he said, "that all was not sweetness, and goodness, and righteousness in the top command. That someone—we've called him a Judas— might give us enough ammunition to persuade Smith and his army inside the Cup that mass murder and perhaps personal suicide was too big a price to pay for two men who had just operated within what you called the System."

"You haven't found a Judas? Not that I think it would work."

"In the beginning our hope was that there'd be something about Paul Kramer, that he wasn't the Great White Father, that he was using their dedication to a cause to make himself rich."

"What nonsense!"

"So you say, and I believe you," Quist said. "But if they thought he had been misappropriating funds, had been laughing up his sleeve at their childish faith in him, they might settle for less out at the Cup. If they were offered freedom from prosecution, they might decide that Kramer wasn't entitled to a bloody revenge for what happened to him."

"Unfortunately for you, that wasn't so," Dyanne said. "I told you why Paul killed Francis O'Brien. I told you why he never told the truth about it. He wanted to protect Milly to the end. But I promise you one thing, Mr. Quist—"

"Julian?"

"I tell you one thing, Julian. Paul was straight as a string. He never did anything, not anything, to betray the trust those people had in him."

132

"You could make it seem he had," Quist said.

She looked at him as though she thought he'd gone out of his mind. "I could do *what?*"

"Would Paul Kramer have gone for the mass murder of three hundred and twenty-five innocent people?"

She seemed to have to consider her answer. "I would have bet my life that he wouldn't," she said finally. "If he thought one of his people had been unjustly convicted of a crime he might have marked down the judge, the prosecutor, a false witness, for death. That would have been the Reaper kind of justice, and he believed in it. But no innocent people. He might have set up a hostage situation to get what he wanted, but he would never have carried through with it if he failed to get the result he was after. He talked to me about it often."

"Hostage-taking?"

"About what he thought was a kind of sickness among some members of the Reapers," she said. "Violence for the sake of violence, bloodletting just for the pleasure of seeing it run. He thought it was a perversion of Simeon Taylor's grim philosophy, 'Sow death, reap death.' He didn't believe that innocent people should suffer for the guilty. He was against bombings that would kill the innocent, against arson that would take lives that didn't touch the problem in any way. He might have approved, in a similar situation, the elimination of Judge Padgett and Carl Zorn. But not your Miss Morton and the others."

"If someone else had given the order to kill innocent people, would he have resisted it?"

"With everything he had, I think. I *know!*"

"Then he would have tried to save those people in the Cup?"

"I think he would."

"If he could save them now by sacrificing his reputation, do you think he would?"

"I don't understand."

"Listen to me, Dyanne. If the Reapers out there in the Cup believed that Paul Kramer had been a fake, a fraud, a thief, would they take less for the hostages—freedom, money? Would they blow themselves to hell to revenge a man who made suckers of them over the years?"

"But he didn't!"

"You could make them believe he had," Quist said very quietly.

"I hope I'm not understanding you, Julian."

"If you were interviewed on the air," Quist said, gesturing toward the TV set, flickering soundlessly through a session of "Family Feud," "by a known newsman, and you told him that Paul Kramer didn't deserve the kind of violent loyalty he was getting from the Reapers; that he had stolen them blind—Swiss bank accounts holding their money; that his shooting O'Brien had nothing to do with the Reapers and their cause, but was purely personal—"

"No! I will not tell Milly's story, I couldn't."

"None of what you would tell the reporter would be true," Quist said. "You could tell the reporter how Kramer used to laugh at what suckers the Reapers are to let themselves be had by a fanatical and phony religious dogma while they were being stolen blind."

"No!"

"It could save those people in the Cup," Quist said. "It can't hurt Paul Kramer. He's gone, Dyanne."

"His reputation isn't something to play games with."

"It could save three hundred and twenty-five lives! You say he would have tried to do that himself."

"I—I could never make it convincing."

"You are an actress," Quist said.

"I'm a singer."

"I have watched you perform—with pleasure. You are a magnificent singer, and with it goes acting to help sell the words you are singing. I think you could convince anyone of anything if you chose."

"How would it go?" she asked after a silence.

"Right now, downstairs in the Trapeze Bar, my partner, Dan Garvey, and Rusty Grimes, a reporter for *Newsview* magazine, are waiting for word from me. They don't know what's in the wind yet. I didn't feel free to lay it out for them till you said yes."

"I haven't said yes!"

It was her last resistance, and he knew it. "There's a lot to do in a very short time," he said. "We must get time on the air. It will be my job to sell one of the networks on preempting programs for the rest of the night. I don't think that's a problem. None of them would want it known afterward that they refused to help those people in the Cup. Dan and I will have to stay out of sight. Through Lydia we're too personally involved. Smith would guess at once that it was a fake. But Grimes has been on the story from the beginning. He would be the reporter who found you, persuaded you to go on television with him."

"Will he be a party to a fake like this?"

"To save over three hundred people?"

"Oh, God, Julian, I won't have a story to tell, won't know how to answer questions in a way that would help."

"That's where Dan and Rusty come in," Quist said. "They'll prepare a story. They'll have cue cards made so that you can read from them on camera if you get lost. But my dear, dear Dyanne, we've got to move at it now, at once!"

She shook her head. "It's madness. I'll fail at it. But if you think there's any chance it could help—"

"Good girl," Quist said, and reached for the phone.

Having something positive to do was a blessing for a man whose fatigue was bone deep. Quist found Dan Garvey and Rusty Grimes waiting in the Trapeze Bar when he talked on the phone to the maitre d', and had them sent up to 1411.

Time trickling away.

It took time for them to come up from the bar, it took time to introduce them to Dyanne, to explain what it was he had in mind. Dan Garvey doubted it would work, Rusty Grimes was more enthusiastic. They both agreed the desperateness of the situation made it well worth trying.

"Smith was way ahead of us on everything else we've dreamed up," Garvey said. "He'll probably smell this out."

"Maybe not," Quist said. "One thing about Captain Haller's technique of containment, Smith's had no way of contacting the outside world since that first hour, before the phones were cut off. It was long after that I first heard of Dyanne and came to see her. There is no way he can know about that, or that I've come back here a second time. Dyanne wasn't in the picture at all during Kramer's trial. If it wasn't for Ossie Lord, I'd never have made the connection."

"At least it will come as a surprise to him," Grimes said. "Now all we need is a script, a story to tell."

"That's for you and Dan and Dyanne to work out," Quist said. "I've got to find us air time."

If there was one thing Julian Quist Associates had, it was contacts with the media. The problem at eight o'clock at night was locating the right person, the person with authority to disrupt a network's programming, to cancel tens of thousands of dollars' worth of advertising. Quist was so deeply involved personally that he hadn't stopped to think that the entire news staffs of all the networks were on the alert, watching events at the Island Complex. It was like Mount St. Helens, belching steam. It could erupt at any time. The top men everywhere had given up their evenings at home, their dinners out on the town, their theaters, their parties. The lives of three hundred and twenty-five people were dangling on the whim of a group of fanatics. That was a potential news blockbuster.

Quist's problem was unique in his career. He had never promoted a personality, a product, a business, an idea in which he didn't believe. What he proposed to do now was promote something he knew to be a total fake.

George Michaels, president of WTN's news division, was an old friend of Quist's, a college classmate. Quist located him in his Madison Avenue office. It took ten minutes for Quist to get there from the Beaumont.

Michaels, a big man with a normally jovial personality, greeted his friend with concern.

"I thought of trying to reach you, Julian, but I decided the best thing to do was stay out of your hair. Lydia?"

"She talked to Dan in the six o'clock contact with the Reapers," Quist said. "I wasn't there, worse luck." His lips twisted in a mockery of a smile. "She told him to tell me that she loves me."

"Of course she does. She's not hurt?"

"Not hurt, not hysterical—she says."

"What can I do for you, Julian?"

"Turn your network over to me for the rest of the night," Quist said.

Michaels, surrounded in his office by a television set, showing a nine o'clock drama show, a news ticker chattering away in a far corner, gave Quist a blank look.

"Try me again," he said.

Quist spelled it out. Rusty Grimes, a reporter with a reputation, would interview Dyanne Jordan, Paul Kramer's long-time girl friend. She would tell a story, not a word of it true, which would discredit Kramer in the eyes of the Reapers who were holding the hostages in the Cup.

"If she can persuade them that Kramer played them for a bunch of suckers, they may back off. If we keep her talking, you may get phone calls from all over the country, other people who may know some real corruption that's taking place in the organization."

"You're asking me to turn over network time to you, watched by millions of people, with a completely phony story?"

"You could save three hundred and twenty-five lives."

"And never be believed again. Our whole reputation is based on 'the truth, the whole truth, and nothing but . . .' et cetera, et cetera."

"And be heroes for saving three hundred and twenty-five lives."

"And if we tried it and it fails?"

"Be heroes for trying. The men who tried to rescue the hostages in Iran died in the attempt. You won't have to die. You just have to let Dyanne tell her story and hope it moves somebody."

"You didn't have to tell me her story was a fake," Michaels said.

"Our friendship is based on 'the truth, the whole truth, and nothing but . . .' et cetera, et cetera," Quist said.

"I'm just talking to cover up the uncomfortable fact that I'm thinking," Michaels said. "When would they be ready?"

Quist glanced at his watch. "You have half an hour to go with this program." He gestured toward the TV set.

"Then five minutes of news, and then a film."

"You could interrupt the film if I can't get them here by five after ten," Quist said.

"It's an old Bogart film. Bogey wouldn't like to be interrupted," Michaels said.

"From heaven he will applaud your motives," Quist said.

Michaels stood up from behind his desk. "I'll buy," he said. "Get your motor running."

A lot of people worked very hard in the next half hour. Only Quist, Michaels, Dan Garvey, Rusty Grimes, and Dyanne Jordan knew they were involved in a fake, a scam of a kind. A studio in the WTN building was readied for a special—cameras, lights, microphones. A simple setting, a table and two armchairs, was set in place. A trained expert was alerted to prepare cue cards if Rusty Grimes wanted them. Telephones for call-ins, with operators to take the calls when and if they came, were rushed into place. George Michaels knew his people, his crews. At a few minutes to ten the network was ready for—whatever.

There was mild resistance to the speed of it from the Beaumont.

"The lady has to change if she's to appear before umpteen million people," Garvey told Quist on the phone. "I thought the more bedraggled she looked the more sympathy she'd get. Rusty thinks the more expensive she looks the more people will be inclined to think Kramer had a little too much money to spend on a broad—for a religious nut."

"You can't turn off that girl's inner light—no matter what she wears or what kind of makeup she puts on her face. I'd say let her choose. She's got a job to do and she shouldn't be worried about anything else."

"She's scared out of her wits," Garvey said.

"That someone may try to strike back at her?"

"Hell, no!" Garvey said. "She's afraid she may fail Lydia and three hundred and twenty-four other people. This is some kind of woman you've come up with, Julian."

"Get her here as fast as you can," Quist said. "The air is ours at five after ten."

Haller was alerted and approved. Anything that might stir up doubts among the Reapers could be a time gainer.

"It would be a disaster if those creeps have gotten tired of looking at their TV set, or are tuned into the wrong wavelength," Quist said.

"I think we can persuade the other networks to carry the same thing, or at least call attention to it," Haller said.

139

"Every newspaper, radio station, and TV station in the country is being flooded by phone calls, demanding action of some kind or another. Right now we *are* the news, just about everywhere in the world. Half the listeners know this Dyanne Jordan as a performer, a star of sorts. I think they're going to believe her."

"I hope she's as good a liar as she is a singer," Quist said.

At exactly ten o'clock Quist found himself in the control booth at the WTN studio along with George Michaels and a young man wearing headphones, who would act as director, or floor manager, or whatever the correct title was for the kind of interview, special, that was coming up. Above eye level in the booth were a series of monitors, each of them covering one camera on the set. There were three of them lighted and active at the moment, focused on the two empty chairs and the table where Rusty Grimes and Dyanne would sit for the interview. Below those monitors was a central one that showed what was actually happening on the network at the moment. A commercial selling the idea that a certain dishwashing soap would make a lady's hands sexually stimulating to her husband was in progress.

Quist was introduced to the young director, Pat Corcoran, by Michaels. "It will be Pat's job to keep the visual part of this interesting," Michaels explained. "One camera will be focused on Miss Jordan, another on Grimes, the third will cover both of them from a little distance back. Each camera will show up, as it does now, on one of those monitors. Pat will select which picture he wants the viewing audience to see, switching from one to the other to give it variety. What he chooses will appear on that main monitor where that soap commercial is showing now. That monitor shows you what the viewers are seeing at all times." Michaels glanced at his watch. "Where the hell are they? Five minutes of news, and then Bogart if they're not here!"

The soap commercial ended and onto the screen came

140

the familiar face of Slim Wallace, WTN's anchor newsman.

"Good evening ladies and gentlemen, this is Slim Wallace with WTN's regular ten o'clock update of the news. All of America and, I daresay, most of the civilized world are concerned at this time with the fate of three hundred and twenty-five hostages being held in the Stirrup Cup restaurant at the Island Complex, famous sports center just outside New York City. As almost everyone must know after almost twenty-four hours of continuous reporting on the situation, the hostages are being held by the Reapers, a notorious religious cult whose motto is 'Sow death, reap death.' The Reapers are demanding that authorities turn over to them Judge Stephen Padgett and Prosecutor Carl Zorn to be executed by them for having participated in the trial, conviction, and sentencing of Paul Kramer, a Reaper of importance. Kramer, convicted of the murder of Francis O'Brien, a government attorney, was sentenced to life imprisonment. He recently committed suicide in a state penitentiary. The taking of the hostages, people who were dining at the Stirrup Cup last night and employees of the restaurant, has now been in progress for nearly twenty-two hours. Skilled negotiators from the Manhattan Police Department have failed, so far, to persuade the Reapers to reduce their impossible demand. Two of the original hostages are no longer in the Stirrup Cup. In the early hours David Fahnestock, a Manhattan attorney, suffering from emphysema and in the throes of a severe attack, was released unharmed. Late today, Joe Lupo, a kitchen helper who apparently offered some resistance when the Reapers first attacked the Cup, died of injuries he received in that encounter and was shipped out by the terrorists in a trash can. We take you now to the Island Complex and Fred Haney."

The picture in the master monitor showed two shadowy figures standing in comparative darkness, the dark outlines of the Cup looming up behind them. Quist felt his aching

141

muscles tighten. Lydia was there, somewhere inside that black shadow.

"This is Fred Haney, ladies and gentlemen, outside the Stirrup Cup at the Island Complex. You're not getting much of a picture in this blackout that has been imposed over the whole area. Normally at this time of night this place would be as bright as day, thousands of people coming and going, thoroughbred horses racing at the track, which is no more than a hundred yards from here. The shadowy building behind me is the Cup. Any other time there would be lights everywhere, along the roof line, in the entrances and windows, coming from floodlights focused on it. There would be people laughing, dining, drinking. You would hear music. Tonight there is nothing. Inside the Cup, after more than twenty-two hours, three hundred and twenty-five people wait, and hope, and perhaps despair. Standing with me here is Captain Jansen of the state police. Captain, why this blackout? Last night, when this first started, the whole area was flooded with light."

"The situation was a little different last night," Captain Jansen said. "Last night we were, of course, caught off guard, unprepared. It was essential for us, at that time, to contain the terrorists in the Cup where they were. Many of the people called in, state troopers, army personnel, were unfamiliar with the terrain, the geography of the Complex. We couldn't have them stumbling around in the dark. Tonight the situation is different."

"In what way, Captain?"

"Tonight all our forces here are thoroughly familiar with the area. We think it's to our advantage to keep the terrorists in the building from knowing exactly where our men are positioned."

"Does that mean, Captain, that your men are in place to attack the Cup if the order comes through?"

142

"You must know, Mr. Haney, that the terrorists inside that building have to be watching every telecast, listening to every radio show, that has any bearing on this situation. I obviously can't say anything that relates to how our men are deployed."

"But an attack is possible?"

"I suppose everyone in the world who's in touch with this situation knows that if negotiations break down between Captain Haller and the terrorists, anything is possible. An attack would certainly be one of our options, but the cost in lives could be pretty shocking. We have until nine o'clock tomorrow morning to come up with some new basis of negotiating with the terrorists. I'd say that any kind of attack before these negotiations take place is most unlikely."

"Thank you, Captain Jansen. And now we take you back to our main studios in New York and Slim Wallace."

Quist felt a hand on his shoulder and looked away from the monitor. George Michaels was pointing out into the studio. Rusty Grimes and Dyanne Jordan were being guided out onto the set by some sort of stage manager or assistant director.

Pat Corcoran, the man in the booth, turned down the sound under the main monitor in the control booth, leaving Slim Wallace an image who could be seen but not heard, his mouth moving in a torrent of words that were inaudible. Corcoran spoke into a microphone that was obviously heard in the studio.

"Hello Rusty—Miss Jordan. Pat Corcoran here in the booth. I will be directing the cameras, lights, and sound for this opera."

Rusty Grimes looked up at the booth and waved. Obviously he and Corcoran knew each other. Everyone ever involved with news knew Rusty.

"Good evening, Miss Jordan," Corcoran said. "It doesn't

143

matter which chair you take, unless you have a good side."

"Side?" Dyanne looked up at him.

Whatever she had done about her appearance, she looked just right, Quist thought. A simple cotton summer dress, a simple gold chain and locket around her neck. Somehow her honey-colored face with its high cheekbones, wide mouth, and deep, dark eyes had a dramatic look to it. She was acting, perhaps unconsciously, already, Quist thought.

"You've done enough work before the camera, Miss Jordan," Corcoran said, "to know whether there's one side of your face you like the audience to see more of than the other. You'll be about three-quarters toward the audience, whichever chair you choose. You like your right side, take the stage-right chair; your left side, the stage-left one."

"I'm a singer, Mr. Corcoran. When I perform I'm not still. I never thought of one side being better than the other."

"Both sides look pretty damn good to me," Corcoran said. "Perhaps the chairs should face a little straighter out, Jerry."

The stage manager moved the chairs.

"Now Rusty, Miss Jordan, you can see the three cameras that will be in use. All three will be going at the same time, but when I select the picture we're using that camera will show a little red light over the lens. That's the camera for you to be looking at. Understand? We'll open with the middle camera—that's number two. That will always pick up both of you. Number one, to your left, will focus on the stage-right chair. That, I take it, will be you, Miss Jordan. Look straight into it when you talk. Number three will be on you in the stage-left chair, Rusty. You've done this kind of thing before."

Rusty made an okay circle with a thumb and forefinger.

"Get settled, please. We have a minute and a half to go,"

144

Corcoran said. "Watch the monitor over this booth. You'll see and hear Slim Wallace announce a change from the regular programming. Watch me, and I'll give you the signal when you're it." He pointed at Rusty. "That'll be the sign, baby. Break a leg."

The large clock in the booth showed a minute to go. Time always moving, moving, moving toward an eventual crisis, Quist thought. He felt a hand on his shoulder again and looked up. Dan Garvey was standing by him.

"We've got a story for her that'll curl your hair," he whispered.

"You don't have to be quiet in here," Corcoran said. "Nothing that happens in here carries out to the public or to the studio out there unless I have my finger on the intercom button. Thirty-five seconds."

"What she has to say will be aimed directly at the Reapers in the Cup," Garvey said. "It won't be an interview for the general public. It will be for them. Her instinct. I think she's right."

"Ten seconds," Corcoran said, his arm raised. "Watch the monitor. It will be Slim Wallace, and then we've in business."

Quist looked back at the monitor. There was the tag end of a commercial for paper towels, and then Slim Wallace, still in the news studio, reappeared.

"Ladies and gentlemen, the film *Treasure of the Sierra Madre*, with Humphrey Bogart and Walter Huston, will not be seen at this time because of an extraordinary news special concerning the hostages being held at the Island Complex. Rusty Grimes, well-known investigative reporter for *Newsview* magazine, will bring it to you. Rusty—?"

Corcoran brought down his arm in a pointing gesture and Rusty Grimes appeared on the monitor's screen.

"Ladies and gentlemen, I am Rusty Grimes. Some of you have seen me on your home screens before. I am told that all three major networks will carry the extraordinary story my guest is about to bring you. For the last twenty-two hours I, like every top reporter in the country, have been focused on the violence that is taking place in the Stirrup Cup restaurant at the Island Complex. Everyone by now is familiar with the hostage story, and with the tragic possibilities of mass murder that go with it. A lady familiar to many of you as one of America's top blues singers has come to me with a story that just may change the demands of the terrorists at the Cup. Here she is ladies and gentlemen, Miss Dyanne Jordan."

"Take number one," Corcoran said. An engineer sitting in front of him pressed a button. Dyanne's lovely face appeared on the screen.

"Take two," Corcoran said. The picture now showed Grimes and Dyanne sitting at the small table.

"You had a reason for coming to me with a story, Dyanne," Rusty said. "Would you mind telling me what it was?"

"There are three hundred and twenty-five lives at stake," she said, in her deep, husky voice. Just the sound of it made you listen.

"Something you know could affect their future, Dyanne?" Rusty asked.

"Take one," Corcoran said.

The camera moved in on Dyanne alone, a semicloseup. She was looking straight into it, straight at whoever was listening. Smith? Quist wondered. Lydia, God help her!

"Everybody has different rules they live by," she said, clear, strong, quite controlled. "I am black. For ten years the man I lived with, when our careers permitted it, was white. Most of you who may be listening to me there in the Stirrup Cup will not be concerned by that. One of the most important and appealing things about the Reapers is the total lack of any racism in their way of thinking. Your organization was founded by a great religious leader, Simeon Taylor, who was black. Over the ten years I just mentioned I came to meet many of you, some black, many white, Hispanic, a few Orientals. I have disagreed with some of your violent approaches to dealing out justice, your 'Sow death, reap death,' credo, for example. But I also have come to know how much good you have done for the underprivileged, the poor, the sick, the old. I know, because the man I loved and lived with for ten years was what you call a Smith, a leader, a top man in your cult." She seemed unable to go on.

"Take three," Corcoran said in the booth.

Grimes appeared on the screen. "You are of course going to tell us his name, Dyanne."

In the booth. "Take one."

Dyanne was back. You could see her take a deep breath, as though she needed it for courage. "His name was Paul Kramer," she said. "That will come as no surprise to you Reapers in the Cup. Paul and I have circulated at some of your meetings; I have sung at fund-raising gatherings for you. Most of you have known me as Paul's woman. That may come as a surprise, even a shock, to some of the television viewers, but not to you, there in the Cup. It has been no secret from you."

Again she seemed unable to go on, and again the cameras switched to Rusty Grimes.

"You were living with Paul Kramer, Dyanne, at the time that he shot and killed Francis O'Brien, a lawyer for the government?"

She nodded. "I was with him the night before. I knew he was going to do it."

"You tried to stop him?"

"In the sense of reasoning with him, yes."

"As we all know, Dyanne, O'Brien was part of a scam, a setup, a frameup, designed to trap Paul in some kind of

147

illegal act and discredit him and the Reapers. We have believed that Paul killed O'Brien because he, and the Reapers where he was by then a top man, didn't think that the System had the right to entrap and entice people into criminal behavior."

"That was the motive implied at the trial," Dyanne said.

"Are you suggesting that wasn't the motive?"

She nodded slowly.

"I know this isn't easy for you, Dyanne—to reveal unpleasant truths about a man you loved very dearly."

"I tell it only because I hope the Reapers holding those hostages in the Cup may realize that they are threatening the lives of hundreds of innocent people and their own lives as well—to get vengeance for a man who didn't deserve their trust and loyalty, doesn't deserve the holocaust they are projecting on his behalf now. Paul—my Paul—Paul Kramer—was a fraud."

"In what way, Dyanne?"

No one in the world, watching that vital woman, could have turned away from their sets at that moment.

"The night before Paul went to Francis O'Brien's office . . . " she began. Quist, listening, knew that here was coming the story that Rusty Grimes and Dan Garvey had invented for Dyanne. The big lie. " . . . that night Paul told me the truth, something I'd never dreamed of before. What the scam, set up by the government, was all about, really, was drugs. Whatever anyone may feel about the use of drugs, they are part of a way of life—particularly the Reapers' way of life. Paul Kramer, one of the top men in the cult, was assumed to be one of the people involved in channeling drugs from the dealers to the buyers inside the cult. You there in the Cup know how it works. Someone in the cult makes the buy from the outside dealer and in turn sells to the users, the little people who have to have it, inside the cult. Theoretically, this eliminated the middle

148

man, the street dealer, making the precious stuff much cheaper for the users in the cult. The government was certain someone must be making a huge graft, a skimoff, by this trade and they assumed Paul Kramer was the man. They posed as drug wholesalers, bucking the mobsters who control the East Coast traffic. To get the business they would undersell the competition, giving Paul a chance to make an even bigger profit for himself. He knew what they were trying to do, he knew it was a scam, and he was laughing at them and keeping them dangling."

"Then he was honest?"

"So far as the drug traffic was concerned," Dyanne said. "Honest in the sense that he was not stealing from his friends—in that area. It was a criminal act, of course, to deal in drugs, but not thought of as a crime by the users, the people in the cult who *had* to be supplied. A way of life."

"Then—?"

"Paul was the chief fund raiser for the Reapers. He traveled from one end of the country to the other, pleading with rich individuals, selling 'the message' to groups and clubs. The amount of money raised would stagger you if you knew the figures. I can't give them to you because there have never been any *true* figures. Paul saw to that."

"Meaning?"

"That night—the night before he shot Francis O'Brien—Paul told me the truth. Contributions were always channeled through him. He had, over the years, abstracted tens of thousands of dollars from those contributions for himself. He had, he told me that night, accumulated a small fortune for himself, which was resting comfortably in numbered Swiss bank accounts."

"He'd never told you this before?"

"No. I would have—he knew that I would have refused to be a partner in it, to have shared even indirectly in it."

149

"But he told you that night?"

She nodded. She was looking straight at the camera. A great actress, Quist thought. She was almost certainly thinking one thing—the brutal rape of Kramer's autistic sister—and saying words that Dan and Rusty had designed for her.

"Francis O'Brien had found out the real truth about Paul," she said. "O'Brien saw gravy for himself. He demanded a cut of what Paul had in the Swiss banks and a share of all new monies that came in. That, or make public what he had discovered. Paul was caught in a vise. He could be bled to death by O'Brien for the rest of his life, or be punished by the Reapers when they learned the truth about him. He chose what seemed to him the only way out: eliminate O'Brien. It would cost him his own life, but the Reapers, his friends, would never know that he'd cheated them."

"But you are revealing this now, Dyanne."

The bright eyes still focused directly at the listeners. "Because I think he would want me to," Dyanne said. "Paul was tempted by money that came into his possession, but he loved the Reapers, loved people. I think if he could see what is happening tonight out there at the Cup, he would step forward and confess to his old friends. He would not want to be responsible for their being involved in a senseless violence against innocent people, that could perhaps cost them their own lives."

"You, who were in love with him, don't think his reputation was worth preserving?" Grimes asked.

"Not at the cost of several hundred lives," Dyanne said. "I don't think Paul would consider his reputation was worth that price."

"Thank you, Dyanne, for this extraordinary story," Grimes said. "I know it has taken courage to tell it."

Dyanne learned forward toward the camera. "Please—

150

out there in the Cup—I really believe Paul would want you to know the truth. There must be ways to resolve the situation there without destroying yourselves. Please, *please* consider them."

Corcoran made a throat-cutting gesture with his forefinger and leaned back in his chair. Slim Wallace appeared on the master monitor and the engineer cut off the sound.

"She did a great job," Dan Garvey said, at Quist's side.

Quist covered his eyes with his hands. They felt hot in their sockets.

A little white light was blinking on and off by the telephone at Corcoran's right. He picked up the phone and answered. Then he held it out toward Quist. "Captain Haller at the Complex for you, Mr. Quist."

Quist took the phone. "Yes, Captain?"

"Nice try, but no cigar," Haller said, in a flat, toneless voice. "Smith was on to me almost before the lady finished."

Quist leaned forward in his chair as though he had a stomach cramp. "And?"

"He was laughing," Haller said. "He said the performance on television was the funniest thing he'd seen since a W. C. Fields movie on the Late Show."

"Oh, brother!"

"He suggested 'that crazy bitch' was probably performing a sketch written by you. 'A clever PR job' he called it. One big problem with it, he told me. 'I handled every contribution that came into the Reapers. I know exactly where it was banked because I did the banking. All my people here in the Cup know that. They've been laughing along with me. What a phony! What a fake!'"

"Well, we tried," Quist said. "Will it hurt things?"

"I'm afraid it won't help," Haller said. "One last thing, which was probably just big talk."

"Some kind of threat?"

"He said he hoped you would be less careless of Miss Morton's safety than you had just been of the truth."

The "rat" was eating away at Quist's gut again. "New deadline?"

"No. Nine o'clock in the morning. But he warned he must have results then or he would begin sending us 'some fresh garbage.'"

"Meaning dead hostages?"

"That's what he meant, Mr. Quist. The pressure to risk a rescue while it's still dark is going to get pretty intense out here."

"For God's sake hold off for a while," Quist said. "The phones are starting to light up like a Christmas tree down here. Somebody may come up with something we can use."

2 It had been done so well. Dyanne Jordan had been so expert at what she'd done. What incredible bad luck that the Smith in the Cup was the one man who could have blown their elaborate invention sky high. Had Smith been anyone else the doubts would almost certainly be rising out there.

There was one possibility, Quist told himself. There was no way for Smith to get his denial of Dyanne's story to the outside. There was no phone he could use except the one that connected him with Haller. Thousands of Reapers on the outside must have watched and listened to the telecast. Phone calls were flooding the WTN switchboard. Someone might come up with something, some piece of information that could be used in a last bargaining in the morning.

In the greenroom outside the studio where the telecast

had taken place Quist met with Dyanne and Rusty Grimes and Dan Garvey. They were stunned by the news he brought them.

"I knew I couldn't carry it off," Dyanne said in a shaken voice. "I've never been a good liar. I knew I couldn't be convincing."

"You were marvelous," Quist said, taking her hands in his. They were ice cold. "It was just awful luck. The one person who could make it all fall apart was there." For just a moment she was in his arms, crying softly.

He looked past her at Garvey and Grimes. All three men were asking themselves the same question. What now? If the police and the army people decided that a rescue attempt must be made now or never, they could turn the Cup into a slaughterhouse. If they waited till after the nine o'clock call in the morning, the chance of surprise would be gone for another twelve hours. In that time Smith could carry out his threat and begin sending out "some fresh garbage." You could argue for the rescue attempt and sound perfectly sane—unless there was someone trapped in there who mattered. They were names or numbers—unless it was Lydia!

"Do you really believe something might come in over the phones?" Rusty Grimes asked.

"One chance in a thousand," Quist said. "But we can't overlook it if it does come. George Michaels is alerting the switchboard girls to take down every chance remark."

"And if there's nothing?"

"If there's nothing, it gets to be Russian roulette," Garvey said, his anger obvious. "Who comes out in the garbage cans?"

"Would you go in if you had the say-so?" Rusty asked.

"Christ, I don't know!" Garvey said. "I'll tell you this, though. If I did, I'd kill every damn Reaper I could lay my hands on."

"Till they blew up you and the building and everyone in it," Quist said.

Round and round.

Dyanne moved out from Quist's protective arm. Tears had passed. "So much of what I said out there was true," she said.

The three men waited for her to go on. Quist had the notion that the pulse he could feel beating at his temples was keeping time with the electric clock in Haller's office—one less second to go.

"Paul did come home from his trips with money, extravagant sums of money. He was brilliant at getting large contributions from wealthy people, and the fund-raising meetings he organized, where spellbinding, rabble-rousing speakers sold the Reapers' message, produced amounts you wouldn't believe—in dimes, and quarters, and dollar bills. These people have a bulging treasury, and much of it does good, I'm sure. Paul would be very pleased with himself when he got back from a trip. The small change that had been collected—wheelbarrow loads, he said—he would have cashed in at a local bank where the rally was held, turned into a cashier's check. There was one phrase Paul used quite a few times. He would wave the checks he had collected at me and say, 'Mickey is going to be very pleased with these.' Or, 'Mickey is going to have to buy us a steak dinner for these.'"

"Mickey who?" Quist asked.

"I've been wracking my brains ever since you brought us the news, Julian. Did Paul ever mention a last name? I swear I can't remember that he did. I knew he was referring to the 'money man' in the Reapers. That he would be passing on the checks to Mickey. But a last name—I'm sure he never mentioned one. Concealing real names was routine. I don't remember any other names but Smith, Jones, and Brown—except Mickey."

"Could be Irish," Grimes said.

"There are a million Mickeys—all named after Mickey Rooney."

"Mickey Smith!" Quist said. "That's what the guy in the Cup just told us. He is Mickey."

"Surely the thousands of members have real names," Rusty Grimes said. "They have to live, work, draw Social Security, or Medicaid, or food stamps. The top people hide behind Smith, Jones, and Brown; but in the ranks there must be real names. The FBI must have real names, the police must have some that Kreevich could find for us. Ask some of them about Mickey and the last name might turn up."

"What are we doing standing around here?" Garvey asked.

"You and Rusty do what you can to find a name," Quist said. "Work with Kreevich and the FBI, check with the telephone operators here at WTN. I'm going back out to the Complex."

"To do what?" Garvey asked.

"I've got to be there to raise my voice in case some idiotic general gives the order to attack the Cup." A muscle rippled along the line of Quist's jaw. "And go in with them if they go in. There's just a chance I could do something to help Lydia."

Summer rain clouds had settled over the area as Quist set out along the express toward the Complex. He had stopped at Beekman Place long enough to collect some rain gear and a handgun for which he had a license.

Part of his problem, in spite of his anxiety for Lydia, was to stay awake. The cone of light he followed, the rhythmic back and forth of the windshield wipers, were almost hypnotic. He tried to visualize the large dining room in the Cup, crowded with the hostages, some blindfolded, some—like Orso's loud-mouthed man—with adhesive tape over his mouth. People under that kind of pressure, twice

155

around the clock, would be stripped of all pretenses. Cool courage and hysteria would be revealed. There would be people, rich people, trying to make their own deals. It must be unbelievable to some of them that there wasn't a price tag for freedom. They must have been aware that the men and women, kids really, who surrounded them with high-powered weapons were being sustained by "speed" or "uppers" or whatever the street names were for the drugs they took. He wondered if Pete Damon, the piano player, who was or had been a Reaper, was trying to keep spirits up with music—like the passengers on the *Titanic* singing as their ship sank into the icy waters. There would be stories afterward—if there was an afterward—of people who had done things to avoid panic that could have triggered violence before there was a chance for safety.

Quist had made this drive out to the Complex many times after dark. As he came closer he kept looking for something that wasn't there, the sky, almost daylight bright, from the thousands of lights that illuminated the racetrack, the arena building, the Cup, the grounds and parking areas. Ahead was darkness. He kept looking for the turnoff, also normally lighted. When he spotted it, leaning forward over his wheel, he saw that the entrance was blocked by several police cars. He had to stop. A trooper, gun drawn, walked up to the driver's side of his car.

"You'll have to turn off your lights," he told Quist. "You don't know what's going on here?"

"I know," Quist said, dimming his headlights.

"Then you must know no one goes in or out, mister," the trooper said.

"I'm Julian Quist. I'm working with Captain Haller."

"I'm President Reagan," the trooper said. "I'm also working with Captain Haller. Just keep rolling on or back the way you came."

"You got a way of communicating with Haller?" Quist asked.

"If I did?"

"Tell him Julian Quist is here and wants in," Quist said.

"Let me see your license."

Quist produced his wallet, containing his license, credit cards, social security card. "If you've been listening for the last twenty-four hours, you'll know that I'm involved," he said.

The trooper nodded. "You got a lady in with the hostages."

"Can you contact Captain Haller?"

"You hold your horses," the trooper said. He walked away, taking Quist's identification with him. A moment later Quist saw the dashlights in one of the police cars go on. He could see the trooper talking on a car phone. After a while the man came back and handed Quist his wallet.

"You seem to check out," he said. "Captain Haller says bring you up."

"'Bring' me?"

"No headlights," the trooper said. "You think you can make it up to the parking area without them?"

"I helped build this place," Quist said. "Why no lights?"

"Psychological, they tell me," the trooper said. "People holding the hostages can't see what's going on outside. This rain's a break, I guess. No moon."

"What's going on outside?" Quist asked.

The trooper shrugged. "Everybody positioned to go in if the order comes. I'm lucky. My job is here, couple of hundred yards away. I never did like the idea of being blown up! Just pull around the last car there on the grass. Don't be surprised if you're stopped again. Someone may not get the word on you."

He wasn't stopped. After a few yards he gave up trying to make it in his car. The darkness was total. He got out and walked. He could feel the blacktop under him. When he strayed off onto grass he found the road again.

Presently he was in the midst of cars in the parking lot

and was oriented once more. The Cup would be just off to
his right, the path to Garvey's office in the arena building
just to the left of that. The rain beat suddenly harder on the
roofs of the cars surrounding him. He almost bumped into
the glassed-in phone booth, but it told him where he was.
A few yards further and a voice came out of the night.

"Hold it right where you are!"

Quist stood still. Someone moved up on him. "I'm Julian
Quist," he said. For just a second a flashlight focused on his
face and was gone again.

"Okay, Mr. Quist. I just had to make sure. I'm one of Vic
Lorch's men. Know you by sight. Vic sent out word you
were on your way."

"Anything stirring?" Quist asked.

"You don't want to stray off the path," the man said, "or
you're likely to stumble over the United States army. Place
is alive with soldiers. Just keep to the left. There's a low
wall there. It'll guide you."

Blindman's buff. The wall did help and after a bit he
was at the building. He went up the two steps to the door
and found it locked, but the moment he knocked it was
opened—to complete darkness.

"Mr. Quist?"

"Yes."

"Come in."

Inside, he heard the door close behind him, and then
there was light. He recognized this man as another of Vic
Lorch's regulars.

"We're not allowed to show any light," the man said,
"Windows are all covered over in here. You look half
drowned. Is it raining that hard?"

"I'm a strong swimmer," Quist said. He took off his hat
and let the water run out of the rim and crown. He glanced
at his watch. Twenty past three.

"Vic's inside with Captain Haller, Mike Romano, and the

158

army. Everybody's in the act, I guess—the mayor, the governor, the White House, the Pentagon. They keep calling Haller every ten minutes giving him advice."

"Who's really in command?" Quist asked.

"There's a macho major in there who might not wait to find out," the security man said. "You can go right in, Mr. Quist."

The office, windows blotted out by black drapes, was thick with tobacco smoke. Haller, looking worn, was sitting at the desk by the telephone. Across from him a man in army uniform with a major's gold leaf on his shoulders was standing, bent forward over the blueprints of the Cup. With him was Mike Romano. The major was verifying every inch of the blueprint plans. Romano, of course, as manager of the Cup, knew the building like his own home. He nodded to Quist, but the major had his full attention.

Vic Lorch was just inside the door when Quist entered. "You find your way through the troops?" he asked. He didn't sound happy.

Haller gave Quist a weary wave of his hand.

The major, a blond Viking of a man, looked up at Quist, scowling.

"Major Huntoon—Julian Quist," Haller said.

"You the public relations man for this place?" Huntoon asked. There was a saw-toothed edge to his voice. He was a chain smoker, his eyes narrowed against the smoke from his cigarette.

"My firm handles the PR work for the Complex," Quist said.

"You pulled that hair-brained stunt with that broad on television?" the major asked.

"It could have worked," Quist said.

"The only thing that matters is that it didn't work," Huntoon said. "It's left us with damned few options, Mr. Quist."

159

"Options?"

"In two hours," Huntoon said, "it will start to be light outside. After that it will be another fifteen, sixteen hours before we can pull any kind of surprise. I'm urging the top brass to let me go in—now, while we have a chance."

"That sounds hair-brained to me, Major," Quist said.

"Oh, does it? Trying to fake them out with a pack of lies seemed sensible?"

"As far as we know the hostages in there are still alive," Quist said. "Mount an attack and God knows how many of them will be dead before you can get a single door or window open."

"But some of them will be alive, which is more than you can hope for if you talk and talk while they chop down their prisoners one by one and send them out to us in garbage cans."

"If the man sitting by that detonator pushed down the plunger they will all be dead, plus fifty-odd Reapers, plus who knows how many of your soldiers, Major; we can only guess."

"I've been trying to find out from Romano where they might have moved that detonator," Huntoon said, turning back to his blueprint.

"Thing is no bigger than a small wastebasket," Romano said. "It could be wired to the explosives from almost anyplace."

"Exactly where did you see the explosives, Romano, when they gave you the guided tour?" the major asked.

"All along the top of the foundation," Romano said, "right under the first floor, the ground level, all the way around the building. The detonator could be attached by a short wire from almost anywhere on the first floor."

"Got to plug it in somewhere," Huntoon said.

"My dear Major," Haller said, "the thing is certainly

battery charged. When you're blasting rock out in the woods you don't have a place to plug in your detonator." The police captain passed a hand over his eyes. "Tell me again, Romano, how it was. They stormed the place just before midnight—night before last. You were where?"

"In my office. The Craven girl and Pete Damon had just finished their second show. I saw her go out to get some air, I guess. Right after the floor show there's a lot of orders from the tables, you know. People were quiet while the girl sang, now everybody wants drinks, sandwiches, whatever. Head bartender asked me for some small bills for a batch of twenties and fifties he'd collected. I went into my office to make change for him out of the safe there. I was bent down, working the safe's combination, when they stormed in."

"Guys in ski masks?"

"And girls," Romano said. "Squealing like pigs! They all had machine pistols, higher than the sky on something, I thought. I was knocked flat on my behind, kicked, and then dragged to my feet and jammed against the wall. Big black bastard had a pistol at my throat. I thought I was going to get it, gangland style."

"How did you know he was black if he was wearing a ski mask?" Huntoon asked.

"His hands, for Christ's sake!" Romano said. "Then I thought he'd asked me to finish opening the safe. There's maybe fifteen thousand bucks there. But he didn't. 'You're the lucky one,' he said. 'Move. We want to show you things.' Well, there was a guy there, boring a hole in the floor. He had that detonator with him, and I watched him push the wires down through the hole he made. Then they took me out of the office. All hell had broken loose in the main dining room, people yelling and screaming and shouting orders. I got just a brief look—dozens of these

161

people in ski masks, waving guns, telling people to sit down and keep still—or else."

"They took you down into the cellar?" Haller asked.

Romano nodded. "Four or five of them. They showed me what I guess are sticks of dynamite, packed neatly around the foundation like cordwood. There was already a guy there connecting the wires that had been pushed down through the floor from my office. Then the big black one took me back upstairs. The one who calls himself Smith told me the score. Hostages—stay away or the whole damn building and everyone in it would be blown away. Security was to stay here, in this office, until they got terms delivered to them. Then they took me out on the back loading platform and kicked me out into the night. I mean literally kicked me." He felt his thigh as if it still hurt him.

"I keep coming back to one sentence of yours," Haller said. "Dynamite, stacked like cordwood. That couldn't have been done in the short time between the breakin and when you were dragged down to see it."

"I know. And they knew exactly where to bore the hole in my office floor to connect their wires," Romano said. "This man Smith reserved his table three days ago—three days before last night."

"Has to be someone working for you, someone who could move around for days in advance, unnoticed," Haller said.

Romano nodded. "Whoever it was is in there now," he said.

"Along with a hell of a lot of important people," Huntoon said, staring down at the blueprint.

Haller picked up some typewritten sheets on his desk, stapled together. "We've compiled a pretty complete list of everyone in there, except, of course, the Reapers. People calling in when someone didn't get home. Three U.N.

162

diplomats makes it international. Romano's given us a list of the help."

"Tell me, Captain," Quist asked, "who makes the final decision about what get's done—negotiate or attack?"

Haller's thin smile was bitter. "Nobody wants to make the decision," he said. "Technically I suppose the town and the county are responsible. But as I've just said, the hostages come from all over the map. The governor—the state—I suppose are next in line. But the State Department in Washington has stuck its oar in because of the UN diplomats. The president is being asked for an opinion, if not an order. The army is here and ready to move if somebody presses the right button."

"And that damn well better happen before we see daylight," Huntoon said.

"What exactly is your base, Captain?" Quist asked.

"New York City Police," Haller said. "I'm supposed to be a specialist at this sort of thing so I get loaned out." Again that bitter smile. "I keep doing my thing until I'm called off."

"The trouble is you've got nothing to negotiate with," Huntoon said. "You can't give them what they want and they won't take anything else."

"So far," Haller said.

"For Christ's sake, you've had twenty-four hours of chitchat with them!" Huntoon said.

"As far as we know all but one of the hostages are still alive," Haller said. "That's not nothing, Major."

"We don't go in while it's still dark and they'll be sending you out one an hour when you come up empty at nine o'clock," Huntoon said.

"Who gives you your orders, Major?" Quist asked.

"The Pentagon, which means the president. Good enough for you, Mr. Quist?"

"You know my woman is in there," Quist said.

"A lot of people's women are in there," Huntoon said. "And husbands, and sons, and fathers. You come down to a point where you have a chance to save some of them—or none of them!"

Someone knocked on the office door and Vic Lorch opened it.

"Coffee and sandwiches," a cheerful voice said.

A man with a table on wheels came in. Quist recognized him as one of the commissary staff in the arena building.

"You gotta eat to keep alive, gents. Best we could do for you in the dark. Turkey sandwiches, coffee, doughnuts." He grinned at Romano. "Your Sanka in the china pot, Mickey. I remembered about you and caffeine."

"Thanks, Tommy," Romano said.

"Mr. Garvey keeps a supply of booze in that closet over there," Tommy said. "I should of brought you some ice and glasses. If you say the word—?"

"When this is over," Haller said, "you can bring us a bathtub for booze."

Quist's whole body felt rigid, frozen. He watched the commissary man leave. He moistened his lips and tried to speak in a normal voice.

"I never heard you called Mickey," he said to Romano.

Romano laughed. "Tommy Conti and I grew up together," he said. "My mother was Irish. My pop named me Michael and called me Mike. My mom compromised and called me Mickey. When I was a kid everyone called me Mickey or Mick. Tommy was one of them."

"And Paul Kramer was one of them?" Quist asked, deadly quiet.

Romano was no actor. A nerve twitched high up on his cheek and his dark eyes narrowed. "I don't know any Paul Kramer," he said.

The terrible anger that had been building up in Quist

164

ever since the taking of the hostages—the taking of Lydia—exploded.

"You sonofabitch!"

He launched himself at Romano, slugging, hammering, pounding at the man with both fists. Romano went down with Quist on top of him. Quist, who had never dreamed of killing a man before in his life, meant to now.

Vic Lorch and Huntoon were the first to get to him, dragging him away. He was standing again, looking down at Romano's bloodied face.

"You gone crazy, Julian?" Lorch said. All three men were breathing hard.

"He's the man who planted all this, who set all this up! He's the money man for the Reapers!" Quist shouted. "That's how the Cup was prepared in advance for them, explosives set in place. Mickey! That was the name Paul Kramer called him. He turned over the money he raised for the Reapers to Mickey! Everything else was arranged in advance. You'll find he has a way to communicate with Smith on the inside. He's been sitting right here in your laps, running the whole show from the outside, knowing what your plans are because you've told him!"

Romano struggled up, wiping at his mouth with a now bloodstained handkerchief. "That bastard is crazy," he said, "I'm getting out of here."

"Not just yet, Romano," Haller said. He had moved away from the desk and was standing in front of the door. The police captain was an imposing-looking figure blocking the way for the small, wiry Romano. "You know something we don't know, Mr. Quist?"

It wasn't a case that would have satisfied a district attorney, Quist realized. All he had was the coincidence of a name. Mike Romano had been called Mickey as a kid and old friends still called him that. The money man for the Reapers had been called Mickey by Paul Kramer. What was it Garvey had said? "There are a million Mickeys, all named after Mickey Rooney." A generation that grew up with *The Hardy Family,* with Rooney, Judy Garland, Lewis Stone, and the others. But there was too much here for it to be a coincidence!

Who could have set up the Cup for a quick takeover better than Romano? He could come and go at all hours of the day or night, unnoticed by normal security because he was entitled to be there. He could have taken days, even weeks, to bring in sticks of dynamite, one at a time, and put them in place for the big moment. He could even have placed a chalk mark on the floor of his office to indicate where a hole should be bored for the detonator's wires. He'd had all the time he'd needed to rig up an intercom system so that he could communicate with Smith from the outside, alerting him to every plan, every speculation, every possible procedure set up by Haller, the troopers, the security men, the army, and the political brass who would make the final decisions.

Finally there was Quist's own instinct in the matter. He had learned to trust what he felt about a situation when he was in a tight spot. It was almost a cliché with his friend Lieutenant Kreevich. "Trust your own impulses when you've got nothing else to go on. They're apt to be right."

He moved his shoulders and Lorch and Huntoon seemed to sense that his homicidal moment was over. They let him go, and for a moment he thought he might drop. Adrenalin down, he had almost no strength left. Killing the bloody-faced Romano wasn't going to free Lydia.

He spoke, finding it almost impossible to get his breath. He told Haller about Dyanne Jordan's story: Kramer returning from a fund-raising trip and waving checks at her. "Mickey is going to be very pleased with these." And, "Mickey is going to have to buy us a steak dinner for these."

"No last name?" Haller asked.

"She couldn't remember that Kramer ever mentioned one."

"And that's all?"

"Put together with everything that's happened here, who else could fit so well? Look at him! The sonofabitch can't hide it! *Look at him!*"

Romano started to laugh, almost hysterical laughter. "How crazy can you get?" he asked them all. "I never heard of Paul Kramer until last night—till those creeps charged in. He's saying I'm a Reaper? If any of those hostages ever get out, they'll tell you I was manhandled, kicked around. They saw it!"

"The perfect alibi," Quist said.

"Oh, brother!" Romano said. "Maybe you go off your rocker when someone you love has her neck on the block—like Miss Morton in there! Maybe that's an excuse for him, but he's just dreaming, I tell you!"

"Don't let him go!" Quist said, his voice rising.

"It's worth a look around," Vic Lorch said.

"For what?" Huntoon asked. "We've got less than an hour before it's too late to go in."

"What Julian said about an intercom system. It's worth looking for," Lorch said. He glanced at the major. "If Julian turns out to be right, you haven't got a chance, daylight or dark, Major."

"Go," Haller said. He was still in charge until a higher authority took over. "Tell the cop on the door to come in."

Lorch left the office and a moment later the plainclothesman who had been guarding the outside hall came in.

"Go over Romano," Haller ordered, "just in case he's loaded."

Romano laughed again and held up his arms in a fake gesture of defeat. "I surrender, dear," he said, quoting a popular song. Quist had heard the Craven girl singing it in the Cup long ago—was it only last night?

"He's clean," the cop said, after he'd frisked Romano.

"Look, let me go to the little boys room," Romano said. "See if I can stop this damn nosebleed."

"Go with him," Haller said to the cop. "Keep him covered, and if he makes a move blow him down."

They watched Romano go out into the hall, the cop behind him, gun drawn.

"I hope that's good enough," Quist said. He dropped down into a chair beside Haller's desk. "That bastard probably has a few million bucks at stake. He'll try anything."

"My man won the department's pistol-shooting contest last spring," Haller said. "Chance for us to talk without Romano here."

"I just don't go along with this. It's too far out," Huntoon said.

"Far enough out to be an impossible bull's-eye," Haller said. "Your Miss Jordan think the Mickey she mentioned was on the take?"

"She didn't say so. He was just the man to whom Kramer turned over the funds he'd collected. 'Wheelbarrow loads of money,' according to her."

"And it went where?"

"Wherever they bank, wherever he banks," Quist said. "He probably skimmed off a small fortune for himself."

Haller was beginning to show signs of wear and tear. The lines at the corners of his eyes and mouth had deepened. "We've been talking from the start about a Judas, a betrayer," he said. "More than twenty-four hours have passed and nobody has even waved a little pinky at us. The story has been everywhere—radio, television, newspapers. Broadhurst has offered a half million bucks for his wife. It's obvious large sums of money can be raised. Not a single soul has suggested he might be able to earn a piece of it."

"Suggesting what?" Quist asked.

"That these Reapers are crazy—on the level, thousands of them. That they really believe what they say they believe. That they aren't going to take any less than Judge Padgett and Carl Zorn for the hostages. So maybe you're right about Romano. But if he believes, what have we got?"

"One of an army of psychotics. We can't hold off," Huntoon said, pounding the desk with his fist.

"The major could be right," Haller said. "Maybe all we're doing is making a choice. The hostages die, all in one big bang, or one by one while we wait out another day."

"While there's life there's hope," Quist said. "If I'm right about Romano—and at this moment I'd bet my last buck on it—there may be a way to put enough heat on him, if he isn't a fanatical believer and is using the Reapers to feather his own nest—"

"If, if, if!" Huntoon said.

Quist turned to face the soldier. "How many men would be involved in the attack, Major?" he asked.

Huntoon looked down at a slip of paper on the desk in front of him. "Eight doors, twenty-three windows in the first attack, backed up by about four hundred others set up in a circle around the building. They'd come in the minute the first shot is fired."

"Suppose the Reapers aren't kidding and the man at the detonator blows the place up when the first shot is fired; how many of your sixty-two first-line men would survive?"

"Depends on where the heaviest load of explosives is located," Huntoon said.

"And you're willing to toss those lives into the pot, too, I take it?"

"This country has knuckled under to terrorists long enough," Huntoon said. "It's time the whole damned world knows we can't be blackmailed and bullied."

"So killing three hundred and twenty-five hostages, fifty-two Reapers, and sixty-two of your men will prove that?"

169

The two men faced each other, hostile, and yet they were on the same side.

"I don't find myself very interested in the world's opinion of me at this moment," Haller said. "My job, as long as I have it, is to get as many people out of that place alive as I can. I don't need to prove my manhood to the world, Major. Let's see how hard it'll be to handle Mickey Romano. It's rough to say this in front of you, Quist, but if I could save three hundred hostages after they'd sent twenty-five of them out to us dead, in garbage cans, I'd feel I'd done better than blow the whole joint up with everyone in it."

"I think I'd have to agree," Quist said, in a flat voice, "even if—" He couldn't finish the sentence. Even if one of the twenty-five was Lydia. Not that, please God, not that.

The office door opened and Romano reappeared, followed by the armed cop.

"Docile as a lamb," the cop said to Haller.

Romano had a paper towel held over his mouth and nose. "Stuck pig," he said. "I think my nose is broke."

"Sit down over there," Haller said, pointing to the chair beside the desk.

"I want to know where I stand," Romano said. "If I'm under arrest, I want my lawyer here. If I'm not, I want to go somewhere and lie down before I bleed to death."

"Is Martin Wilshire your lawyer?" Quist asked.

"Never heard of him," Romano said.

"Wilshire says he was hired to defend Paul Kramer by Smith," Quist said, "and paid by Brown. Mickey is the money man for the Reapers, maybe he was Brown. Maybe Wilshire could identify him for us."

Romano looked undisturbed. If Wilshire was his lawyer, Quist thought, he wouldn't identify him.

"So, what am I charged with, Haller?" Romano asked.

"Long as my arm when it comes to it," Haller said, "starting with accessory to the murder of that kitchen helper, and going on to kidnapping, terrorizing, planting explosives, threatening to murder, and on and on. The district attorney will have more legal terms."

"So what are you holding me for? Which one?"

Haller gave him a grim smile. "You're in protective custody," he said. "Quist might finish you off if I turned you loose."

"Joke," Romano said.

"I promise you one thing, Romano," Quist said. "If Miss Morton doesn't come out of there alive and unhurt, you can count on it."

"Big talk," Romano said. "How long are you guys going to play with this crazy idea that I got something to do with the Reapers? I live here, I work here, I've run the Cup for five years, day and night. I've done a good job, which Quist could tell you if he's got enough brains left to remember any facts."

"You're a good electrician, too, Mike," a cold voice said from the doorway. They hadn't heard Vic Lorch come back. His eyes glittered, fixed on Romano. "Under this office is a utility room. Attached to the wall there is a nice, new intercom phone. I pressed the button and picked up the receiver. A voice said, 'Mickey? Smith isn't here. I'll get him for you.' When did you install it, Mickey? Is the other end of the line in your office in the Cup? You bastard!" Lorch took a threatening step forward and then stopped. "I didn't really believe it, Julian, but it was worth a look. This jerk has been stooging for them from the very start! He's the Mickey the Jordan dame was talking about, all right."

"So now you know what the charge is, Romano," Haller said.

Romano took the paper towel away from his mouth and nose. His dark eyes were narrow slits. A little trickle of blood ran down his chin from the corner of his mouth.

"You shouldn't have made that call, Vic," he said.

"They'll know for sure inside that something is wrong out here. Let's hope it doesn't cost you too much."

"Are you in a position to deal, Romano?" Haller asked.

His cut mouth made it difficult for Romano to smile, but he smiled. "Hell, man, I *am* the dealer," he said.

"And Smith?" Haller asked.

"In charge inside," Romano said. "He takes his orders from me. It may be easier after all, Captain, talking to you face to face."

It was a shock to realize that every plan they'd tried to formulate, every option they'd discussed, had been made in the presence of their number one enemy, equipped to pass along everything that could matter at all to Smith, in command of the action for the Reapers. One thing Romano must have learned in this long twenty-four hours and more of painful bargaining was that the Reapers' primary demand would not be met. Not one person, at any level of power from the president on down, had considered for a moment turning over Judge Padgett and Carl Zorn as ransom payment for the hostages. It wasn't being considered at this crisis moment by anyone at all, not even by Quist, who would have given his own life to get Lydia away from the terrorists. Major Huntoon had come the closest.

"The Israelis have the right idea about this kind of situation," he'd announced at some point. "They won't deal with terror! They just won't deal. If that bloody-handed Arafat takes hostages and makes demands for the freedom of what he calls 'political prisoners,' the Israelis write off their own people—their *own people,* mind you—as dead soldiers in a war. They attack, rescue if possible, but pay nothing, give nothing."

"And the terrorists bomb school buses and airports, killing innocent women and children," Haller had responded. "It *is* a war, Major, this isn't. The Israelis and the

Palestinians are fighting over territory, over national boundaries, political control. It's a war over a war. Here we have sick fanatics demanding a sick revenge for a perfectly legal action by the courts."

Do nothing but talk, Quist thought, and the hostages will wind up as "dead soldiers," one by one. Attack and they will all be "dead soldiers" in a few minutes' time. He had thought during the early hours of this dreadful night that there would be a way to disillusion the terrorists in the Cup, to persuade them to ask for less than they were demanding. Watching Romano, Mickey Romano, he thought there must still be an out. This slippery little man, he was certain, was no religious fanatic fighting for a different Ten Commandments, set up by a dead, black preacher. This was a man raised as a shrewd, tough street kid. He had managed the Cup since the Complex had opened for business five years ago. He had proved himself to be a clever buyer, an efficient manager of a difficult staff, producing a handsome profit for his employers, almost certainly making an extra dollar for himself here and there. Romano, preaching the Simeon Taylor Gospel to a bunch of sick kids, was hard to imagine. Everything suggested he was a man out for himself, not for a cause. How did you deal with him now that he was out in the open? He still seemed to hold all the aces.

"So deal, Romano," Haller said.

"It's very simple," Romano said. It hurt him to smile, but he still smiled. "Deliver Padgett and Zorn to us and we'll release the hostages—after we're satisfied that you've provided a safe way out for my people, the judge, and the prosecutor."

"You know, perfectly well, that there is no way we can deliver those two men to you," Haller said. "A way out—to any place in the world you name—is possible. Money, which I suspect is really what you want, is possible. What else?"

"You ship us out of the country, and we'll need money, for sure," Romano said.

"How much?"

"It isn't worth talking about yet," Romano said. "First there must be the judge and the prosecutor."

"The bastard doesn't understand English!" Huntoon said. "That's not possible, Romano, and you know it. Why not lay it on the line?"

"It'll be laid on the line for you, any minute," Romano said. "When Smith knows that call on the intercom wasn't from me, he'll have a new set of demands for you. I told you, Lorch, it was a mistake to make that call."

"When we talk about money, Romano," Haller said, "we could be talking about a small fortune."

"Which we'll be allowed to spend in Libya? I think not, Captain. Those people in the Cup are believers. They want to exact just punishment for the death of a beloved comrade. They're not looking for a good time in Disneyland."

The telephone on the desk rang. The call could only come from one place on that line, the Cup.

Haller pointed to the squawk box, made a gesture for silence and picked up the phone. "Haller here," he said.

The mocking voice of Smith came out through the squawk box into the room. "I'd like to talk with Mike Romano, the Cup manager," he said. "I suspect he's there with you. Some things in here aren't working properly and I need him to tell me what to do."

"You know this is an open call, Smith. Everyone here in the office can hear it."

"Romano will have the right answers," Smith said.

Romano didn't have to move from where he stood to speak. "I didn't make the call," he said.

"I thought not," Smith said. "They know?"

"But not what to do about it," Romano said.

"They harmed you in any way?"

"A little rough handling," Romano said.

"What do I do?" Smith asked.

"Step it up, friend. Step it up," Romano said.

"Are you there, Captain Haller?" Smith asked.

"I'm here," Haller said.

"You seem to have forced our hand, Captain. The nine o'clock call still stands. But don't bother to make it if you haven't got the judge and Zorn ready for delivery. After that we'll send you out a hostage every half hour—in a trash can."

"One body comes out and you all go!" Huntoon shouted.

"Your choice to make, Major," Smith said. "You'll have to live with it. I won't."

The dial tone came through the squawk box loud and clear.

"That crazy freak!" Huntoon exploded. "Will he really let himself be killed?"

"There's a way to find out, Major," Romano said. "Just keep playing it stupid."

The impulse to take out their terrible frustration on Romano was almost irresistible. Huntoon turned his back on the dark little man with the bloodied face. Quist looked down at his fists. He'd already traveled that road and produced no results. Vic Lorch moved restlessly up and down, muttering to himself. Only Haller seemed to take it in stride. Perhaps it was a kind of discipline learned in dealing with endless crisis situations. You acted as though it was everyday. Now he had produced a caked briar pipe from his pocket and was filling it from a plastic roll-up pouch. A quiet after-dinner smoke with a friend?

"Try your coffee, if it's still hot enough to drink," he said to Romano. He poured some for himself, sipped it, nodded, held a match to his pipe. All the time his eyes studied Romano, thoughtfully. "The stupidest thing about

175

us—about me, at any rate," he said, "is that I haven't guessed what it is you really want, Romano."

"The stupidest thing about all of you is that you don't believe what I keep telling you," Romano said. "We want two men delivered to us, not later than nine o'clock this morning."

"I know people, Romano," Haller said. "My job. I have to make judgments about them, how their minds work. If I was wrong very often, I'd be out pounding a beat somewhere. I think I know you."

"If you did, you'd know we're not bluffing," Romano said.

"I'll bet my badge on it," Romano said. "Because you're not some freaked-out religious nut locked up in a monastery somewhere. You're a city-raised kid, sharp, with a knowledge of how to deal with people yourself. You've been handling people—the job here at the Cup for five years—in a first-rate fashion. You've handled a large temperamental staff and thousands of demanding customers. You've never been isolated, focused on some cult-type way of living. You have the brains to run a big business, to run a corporation, to be a politician—whatever you choose. You've chosen to be a crook and a con man." The captain said that last without any emotion. It was as if he were reading a fact out of an almanac. "You see more money in that for you, more power, than in following the conventional route."

"You ought to write a book on me, Captain," Romano said.

"I may just do that when this is over," Haller said. "I'll have all the answers then, won't I?"

"You've got the answers now, Captain. You know what we want, and you know what'll happen if we don't get it."

Haller tapped down the tobacco in his pipe with his

forefinger and puffed contentedly. "I've got the answers now," he said, "except the main one. We know, from Kramer's lady friend, that you have been the money man for the Reapers for quite a long time. Kramer talked about turning over funds to you. Part of that time—the last five years—you've been running a full-time job here. We'll know, sooner or later, what you've done with Reaper funds that were turned over to you. Half of them go to you? More than half? You've had an army of crazed people who can be used to blackmail, threaten, even kill if they are ordered to do so. That's power for an ambitious man like you, Romano. Part of my book will have to be about how a smart street kid persuaded the Reapers that he could be one of them, believe as they believe, help provide the funds necessary to keep them afloat, take care of their poor, their jobless, their old and sick. You must have made them believe you are some kind of a hero. In a way I suppose you have been. But now, the way I read it, you're making your big play. You had control of the Cup. Hundreds of rich and famous people were in your hands every day. You could make the hostage strike to end all hostage strikes. You could demand almost anything you wanted to get them released and get it. And yet you ask for the one thing, the only thing, a civilized society won't give you, can't give you: the lives of two men. Now I can understand how a band of religious fanatics might believe such a deal is possible. High on 'speed' or whatever they take to keep them in high gear, they might believe anything. But not you, not Mickey Romano, the slick kid from the Lower East Side. You're not on uppers. I've watched you twice around the clock, friend. You're not on drugs. You say you're the dealer, you call the game. You know, without taking a deep breath, that we can't give you the judge and Zorn. You're asking for more than we can give to make certain we'll come through with what you're prepared to accept. That's standard dealing, isn't it? So what is the price, Romano? I'm prepared to be shocked, but what is it?"

"The judge and Zorn," Romano said, still smiling.

"There are two ways to deal with this creep," Vic Lorch broke in. "Let Huntoon put him in the front line when he attacks. Let him be shot down by his own people. Or turn him over to me."

"You, Vic?" Haller asked.

"Out there in the dark, beyond Huntoon's soldiers, are hundreds of people who work here at the Complex; maintenance people, horse people who work in Shed Row, people whose jobs and living depend on this place operating. Let them have this guy who's put them out of business for just ten minutes—!"

"You can't do that, Captain," Romano said, still smiling, undisturbed. "That would be the same as turning the judge and Zorn over to us. And anyway, it wouldn't get your hostages free."

"'Sow death, reap death.' That's your motto, isn't it, Romano?" Lorch asked.

"But you don't believe in it," Romano said.

"I'm getting there fast," Lorch said. "I'm like Julian. One hostage gets hurt and you get to be a life's work with me, buster."

"So what is the price?" Haller said quietly. "I can't urge Major Huntoon to hold off much longer. There'll be fewer people killed in the dark than there would be in the daylight. Maybe that's the only thing I have to consider."

"No!" Quist heard himself whisper.

"You turn me loose, I've got the authority, Captain," Huntoon said.

Haller leaned forward and knocked out his pipe in an ashtray. "Last chance, Romano," he said. "Tell me what you'll really take, or I'm off the case."

Romano looked shaken for the first time. "The Reapers have set the price. I'm just their agent."

"Then talk them out of it," Haller said. "Persuade them to take less and give up the impossible. Money we can find. Freedom to get away we can provide."

"You're wasting time, Captain," Huntoon said. "Another hour and our chances thin out."

"You haven't got a chance, soldier man," Romano said.

"Nor have you, buster," Vic Lorch said. "Count on that."

There had to be still another way, Quist told himself. Attack and boom—the end of the world, the end of his world with Lydia there.

"You've maneuvered yourself into quite a position, Romano," he said. "If the army goes in and most of the hostages are killed, you've got real problems. I'll be gunning for you, if Luigi Orso's people are hurt, he'll be gunning for you, and when the Reapers learn that you've been stealing them blind for years, they'll be gunning for you. There won't be anyplace for you to hide. There won't be anyplace for you to spend the money you've stolen. Where is it, Swiss banks? Just spread around the city in different banks? When it's all over we'll have plenty of time to make a case out against you."

"There's not a damn thing you could ever prove in court," Romano said.

"I don't want to prove it in court," Quist said. "I just want to be able to prove it to the Reapers. They won't need a court case to punish a Judas, will they? Because that's what you are, Romano, a Judas. We've been looking all over the map for a traitor and all the time we've had him right here in the room with us."

"So I feathered my nest a little, but I kept them in business," Romano said. "They owe me."

Haller leaned forward and opened the drawer of his desk. "Boy, it's been hard to get you to say something like that, Romano. I hope this damn thing works." From the drawer he produced a small tape recorder. He pressed the rewind button and then the play button.

Quist's voice came through, loud and clear. *"There won't be any place for you to spend the money you've stolen. where is it, Swiss banks—?*

"You had no right to tape our conversation!" Romano said, his voice shaken.

"Works fine," Haller said. He picked up the telephone. "I think Brother Smith may be interested to hear it all."

"No!" Romano cried out. He made a charge for the tape recorder.

Vic Lorch was too quick for him. The big security man caught him, lifted him, quite literally, into the air and threw him against the wall.

Smith's voice came through the squawk box. There's not much point in making new offers, Captain. You know what we must have."

"I haven't got an offer," Haller said. "I just want you to listen to a conversation we've just taped in here. It's between Julian Quist and Mickey Romano. Worth your while, I think, to hear it."

Quist's voice with the lead-in again. *" . . . Where is it, Swiss banks? Just spread around the city in different banks? When it's all over we'll have plenty of time to make out a case against you."* Then Romano's voice. *"There's not a damn thing you could ever prove in court."* Then Quist again. *"I don't want to prove it in court. I just want to prove it to the Reapers. They won't need a court case to punish a Judas, will they? Because that's what you are, Romano, a Judas. We've been looking all over the map for a traitor and all the time we've had him right here in the room with us."* And then Romano. *"So I feathered my nest a little, but I kept them in business. They owe me."*

Flattened against the wall Romano shouted at the top of his lungs. "It's a fake, Smitty! A fix! They're just trying to—"

Lorch struck him across the mouth with the back of his hand. "Shut up, clown, and listen!" he said.

"Find that at all entertaining, Mr. Smith?" Haller asked almost casually.

There was a dead silence in the office. Smith didn't reply for what seemed a very long time. When he did speak his voice had lost all of its sardonic undertones.

"There's a very smart lady in here," he said, "who's been trying to convince me that there was something rotten in Denmark. I'd like to be dead sure of it, Captain. Send in Romano and Quist and give me a few minutes with them. Maybe after that we can do business."

"You can't do that!" Romano shouted. "They'll just hold one of their kangaroo courts and we'll be dead!"

"I'll come in with Romano," Quist said.

"Your Miss Morton will be proud of you, Quist," Smith said. "She's the smart lady I was talking about. The loading platform in five minutes, Captain Haller. We'd better come to some kind of decision before your chocolate soldier in there thinks he sees the sunrise beginning."

Dial tone.

"Romano's right, you know, Julian," Lorch said. "They'll probably hang you both from the center chandelier."

"You're cops! You can't send me in!" Romano said. "That'd be just the same as turning over the judge and Zorn!"

"Four minutes," Quist said. "We're going in to negotiate, Romano. We're the only ones who can."

It was still pitch dark, raining quite hard, when they walked across the rear yard to the loading platform. Quist walked, Romano was carried bodily, protesting by Lorch and two of his security boys. Huntoon was with them. His flashlight picked up two soldiers just outside the rear door.

"We go in, Major?" one of them asked.

"Not just yet," Huntoon said. "Quist and Romano go in. But be ready, in case they pull a fast one."

Lorch knocked on the rear door. Smith's voice answered instantly. "I've got two men with machine pistols aimed at the door," he said. "Anyone but Quist and Romano tries to come in and you get the whole load."

"We're here," Quist called out. "It'll be just us, Smith, but Romano may need to be helped in. Don't misunderstand if there's a third person helping."

"Here we go," Smith said.

The sliding door opened. Beyond it were lights, bright lights. Quist had Romano by one arm, Lorch by the other. He was hanging, dead weight, knees bent. Quist caught a glimpse of two armed men wearing ski masks. He and Lorch heaved Romano through the door and Quist followed him in. The heavy door slid shut. Romano lay where he'd been thrown, arms covering his head, whimpering.

"Welcome to Terror Town, Mr. Quist," Smith's voice came out of the shadows.

He was wearing a rumpled dinner jacket, black tie loosened. He had dark hair, very bright black eyes, a faint stubble of beard growing on cheeks and chin, and a toothpaste-ad smile.

"So our Mickey didn't want to come, eh?" he said. There was a look of disgust on his face as he looked down at the groveling Romano. He gestured to one of the ski-masked gunmen, who with his companion, dragged Romano down a narrow corridor toward the main section of the building.

"That was quite a stunt you pulled with that Jordan broad on television," Smith said.

"We were trying to convince you, you were being had," Quist said. "We didn't have the truth then; we have it now."

"That's what your Miss Morton suggested," Smith said. "She's a nice lady, Quist. I'd hate to have the army blow her to pieces."

"That's why I'm here," Quist said. "To prevent that from happening."

"You didn't think we'd just chop you down for playing games with us?"

"You want something. I'm here to help us come up with some answers—before daylight," Quist said.

"That's simple. Deliver us the judge and Carl Zorn."

"If you've been talking to Lydia, you must surely know how impossible that is. She'd have made that clear to you. I'd like very much to see her."

"First, some plain talk," Smith said. "There's a place here in the kitchen where we can sit down." He opened a side door and walked into the kitchen, brightly lit, aluminum pots and pans gleaming. There was a small table in one corner where kitchen help could pause for coffee or a snack. There were no kitchen people here now. The place was deserted.

Quist sat down at the table. He needed to sit. His legs felt weak under him. "There are so many demands that can be met, Smith, except the one you're asking. Money, freedom, what else is there?"

"Justice," Smith said. "There's one thing Haller and the rest of you don't understand. You think we're some kind of bandits who can be bought. We want only justice, and we mean to get it."

"You say you've talked to Lydia, that you find her a nice lady. She's done you no harm. You're prepared to see her die to get what you call justice?"

"There seems no other way to be heard," Smith said. "I suggested that you come in here so that you could know what we are, who we are. You're wasting time and risking lives because you don't believe."

"If you can convince us, you'll send us out with the message?"

"I might send you out, Mr. Quist, not Romano. Romano is one of us, and he'll have to stand or fall with us."

"How did you happen to trust him? He's no believer, for God's sake!"

"Mickey's father, Nick Romano, was one of our founding members. A great man. He died fighting for justice in a small southern town. Some bastards wearing white sheets hung him from a tree. He brought Mickey in. That was good enough for us. Mickey was a genius at fund raising. We need money for thousands of members, many of them jobless, sick, victims of prejudice and discrimination, victims of the System that uses men like Judge Padgett and Carl Zorn to do their dirty work. So Mickey has been stealing from us and he must pay for it. But that doesn't alter the reason why we're here."

Quist realized that this man believed what he was saying.

"Paul Kramer murdered a man, in front of witnesses. He allowed himself to be arrested. Surely you don't resent a System that has laws against murder. You yourself have laws. 'Sow death, reap death.' In the way that was originally meant, I believe in that, too."

"The System tried to frame Paul," Smith said.

"Paul Kramer didn't kill Francis O'Brien because he was being framed," Quist said.

"Why else?"

"He killed O'Brien because he was an animal," Quist said. "Did you know that Kramer had an autistic sister—a beautiful girl twenty-two years old but she was like a child of four? Looking for facts about Kramer, O'Brien found himself with the girl, alone. He beat and raped her, left her in shock for life. That's why Kramer killed him. He told only one person about this, because he didn't want his sister shamed and jeered at the rest of her unhappy life. Kramer may have been a hero to you, but he gave up his life for personal reasons, not for your cause."

Smith was frowning. "You can prove this?"

"Given time. Dyanne Jordan, Kramer's woman, told me

only tonight. She had no reason to lie. But the sister exists, living with foster parents. The story can be substantiated."

"The Jordan girl was willing to lie about Paul on television?"

"Because she felt she had to protect Paul's sister. She was equally certain that Kramer would have tried to tell you that he hadn't died a hero for the Reapers' cause. He had committed a murder for very personal reasons. You shouldn't risk your lives for that. He cared for you, believed like you. Like you, he was against the System, but he wouldn't want you killing innocent people and yourselves for the wrong reason."

Smith was silent for a moment. "Would the Jordan girl come out here, tell us her story face to face, risk going down the drain with all of us?"

"I think she would," Quist said. "Paul's sister is protected. But it will take time to locate her, time to get her here."

Smith stood up. "I'll give you time if your crazy major will give us time."

"Let's go talk to Haller," Quist said.

The telephone to Haller was in what had been Mike Romano's office. There was no man with a detonator there, but a ski-masked Reaper sat by the phone. In the background Quist could hear the hum of voices, hundreds of voices of people crowded together in the huge dining room. He could hear a woman crying hysterically.

Smith picked up the phone, dialing an extension. "Captain Haller? Talk to Mr. Quist, please."

Quist took the phone. "I think I've persuaded Smith there are facts he should know," he said. "I need Dyanne Jordan to back me up. Get Mark Kreevich to bring her out here as fast you can. Smith will hold off if Huntoon will hold off."

"You believe him?"

"Yes."

"You're not saying this with a gun at your head?"

"No."

"If the girl doesn't want to come?"

"Tell her it will cost lives, mine included."

"They're holding you?"

"No, but I'll stay here with Lydia."

"You've seen her?"

"Not yet."

"What will Smith ask for if the Jordan girl can convince him of something?"

"Let me put him on," Quist said, and handed Smith the phone.

Haller asked his question.

"It's simple, Captain," Smith said. "If what the Jordan girl tells me is satisfactory, I want a free way out for all my people here. No money. I've told you that from the start. I'll keep a half dozen hostages till you get us to a safe place. Can you persuade the army to cool its heels?"

Apparently the answer was yes. Smith put down the phone. "You believe in Haller?" he asked.

"All the way down the line," Quist said.

"So, we wait," Smith said. "You heard me say we'd keep a half dozen hostages. Maybe you, the Jordan girl, Miss Morton. You'd better be right about Haller. Now, you want to see the animals in the cage? It would shock you, Quist, to know how people act under pressure. We've been offered a fortune in bribes, women bartering their flesh for freedom. 'To hell with the guy at the next table, just free me.' The Reapers believe in something. These people don't believe in their System. They only care about themselves. I'm proud of my people, fanatical as they may seem to you."

Smith led the way across the entrance hall to the doors of the dining room. It was a sight Quist couldn't have imagined. People crowded together, surrounded by armed

186

kids in ski masks. The air thick with tobacco smoke. Faces drawn, haggard; men unshaven, women with smeared makeup. There was the crying woman he'd heard from the hall. There were three men with adhesive tape over their mouths, hands tied behind their chairs. Orso's men, Quist imagined.

Seeing him in the doorway with Smith, voices rose and several people cried out to Quist. He didn't pay attention. At a far corner table he saw Lydia, serene, lovely. He started toward her—"across a crowded room," as in the song.

He stopped a foot or two from the table. "Good morning, Miss Morton," he said.

"Good morning, Mr. Quist," she said.

"You look lovely," he said.

"You look dreadful, Julian, if you don't mind my saying so. Is there a chance?"

"I think so. At least we'll be taking it together."

"That I like," she said.

"Would you mind, very much, Miss Morton, if I were to kiss you in public?" he asked.

"Very frankly, Julian, I'd be outraged if you didn't."

And so he did. And then they sat down together to wait. Somehow the passing of time didn't matter any more.